SUMMER NIGHT, WINTER MOON

SUMMER NIGHT, WINTER MOON

a novel by Jane Huxley

DELANCEY PRESS
LONDON 2007

Published by Delancey Press Ltd.
23 Berkeley Square
London W1J 6HE

www.delanceypress.co.uk

A CIP catalogue record for this title is available from the British Library.

First published 2007

Edited by Alexandra Shelley
Painting by Peregrine Heathcote
Jacket by Michal William
Typeset by BookType
Printed and bound by WS Bookwell

ISBN 978 0 9539 1195 0

The heart has reasons
that reason knows
nothing about.

Blaise Pascal
Pensées.

But you, the reader, will look
beyond reason to understand,
and no doubt you will.

J. H.

CONTENTS

ONE

June 21, 2005

It is not unusual, on a warm summer evening, to look out of our bedroom window and see a Jaguar or Corniche parked downstairs in front of my gate on Chester Crescent. What struck me as odd was the vehicle which had just arrived – a black sedan such as a mortician might favour. Or a clandestine lover. Or a copper.

Since I was not expecting a visitor on this ordinary Tuesday evening, the presence of a strange car at my door was an obvious source of anxiety – made worse by the fact that the car doors opened and two men climbed out. Plain clothes that wouldn't fool anybody. Least of all someone with a queasy conscience.

By the reddish glow of the setting sun, I saw one of them lift his head and stare at the façade of the townhouses that form a wide curve along the street. Good Lord! None other than Inspector Fielding himself! Those snake eyes of his darting swiftly as if afraid of losing their prey.

I had forgotten him the way we forget people we have no desire to remember. But if I wanted to reacquaint myself with him, he was giving me ample opportunity. Tall. Narrow head. Abrupt gestures that were part of the art of intimidating suspects.

He stepped forward under the streetlamp and chatted to his partner, whose dense silhouette I recognized as that of Sergeant Dale. Shorter. Plumper. More reticent. Less alert.

They both glanced at their watches, then focused their attention on my house. The black door, the windows upstairs, the small garden in front. Illogically, I wanted to stay welded to the window which might have given away the outline of my head had the lights not been switched off.

The buzzer rang two minutes later.

What's two minutes in the life of a thirty-six-year-old man? A fucking lifetime, if you've ever looked out of your window and had a flash of insight that revealed you were about to be nailed for a heinous deed. So it's a question of choice. You can let them cuff you and throw you into that swamp between nowhere and no place. Or you can pull yourself together. And bolt.

Now you listen to me, you fool, I said to myself. *Who cares if those detectives waiting outside the door will sniff a touch of guilt in a fleeing man. What may look like a fugitive to them will be nothing more than a disciplined jogger to those who pass him along the way.*

But I had two concerns – money and identification – without which an ordinary joe doesn't cross many boundaries in today's world. It would be unwise to stop at the gallery and take whatever bounty was stored in the safe. So I opened the lockbox camouflaged by the small Matisse on the bedroom wall and took out wads of pounds, bounded and crisp, and my passport, and stuffed them in the breast pocket of my jacket.

Not enough. I must take something of hers. Something I can carry with me all the way to wherever I end up. Yes! Her handkerchief. The small white one, with the A embroidered on a corner and the lingering lemony smell.

As I plucked it from her drawer, the mirror on the dressing table gave me a startling look of myself. The thick blond hair, spiky and dishevelled. The forehead shiny with perspiration. The grey eyes, ordinarily amused, wide open and red rimmed. One side of the mouth turned down in a smirk. The hint of a stubble on my cheeks. As for the rest of me, not much left of the slender carriage – I was all slumped shoulders and fidgety hands.

The buzzer rang again.

Come on, you fool, I muttered under my breath. *Run!*

Which is what I did. I rushed to the back of the house and attempted to lift the guest room window that let onto the fire escape. Damn! Stuck so badly only a ghost could pass through it. Now what? A hammer. A rock. Anything.

I found a boot and banged the frame to force the window open. It did, giving me the feel of summer air. I took a deep breath and jumped out for the long run to... Where? Onward, obviously. As far as I can get. The boundless lands of New Zealand, maybe. To what use? To move on, to leave no traces. Why? To preserve whatever part of me is salvageable. If any.

TWO

June 19, 2005

The phone in the library rang over and over and still I hesitated to answer, knowing it was the sound of Dante's angry panic.

"Damn it, Trev," his voice exploded in my ear when at last I picked up. "Get down here. Now! You've got to see me through this."

So I said I would. And that's why I found myself in this appalling building, groping for keys and coins before I passed through the metal detector, then rode a joltingly slow lift to a third-floor chamber marked CONSULTATION ROOM, as if anyone could possibly doubt that this garishly lit, funereal vault could be anything but a Custody Area.

Unless you have been charged in a crime, it is not easy to comprehend the rituals of incarceration. So I assumed an air of aplomb and approached an officer with an inquisitive glare.

"Danilo Terranova," I said.

He scanned his computer and enquired if the person in custody might call himself Dante.

"That's him," I said.

"Are you a solicitor?"

"Yes," I lied.

The stern eyes speculated about how best to use his own scraps of authority. "Wait," he ordered.

While he punched buttons and studied the numbers on his screen, I was left sitting on a metal chair. Too late, as usual, I attempted to block the image of two boys, Dante and me, growing up together in a middle-class neighbourhood of West Palm Beach, Florida, on the crossroads of Tangerine Road and South Dixie. We both lived in white stucco houses in the shadow of a luxury apartment building draped in bougainvillea and surrounded by giant Australian pines that thrust their spindly tops at the brilliant blue sky.

We each had a parent. Mine was a disgruntled father who consumed a quart of Jack Daniel's every night in order to blunt his frustrations as an abandoned husband, single parent and flood-insurance salesman. Dante's, in contrast, was a sexy, youthful mother, with pin-curled bleached hair, lacquered lips and nails, an hourglass figure and slinky necklaces draped over her décolletage.

I had been dumbfounded to hear the neighbours say that her splashy "affluence" owed nothing to inheritance but, rather, to her brazen bluffs in high-stakes poker games (a subject I chose never to discuss with Dante since it was neither useful nor gallant to blurt out unsavoury bits about his mother).

Not surprisingly, in the end, it was my father who drove off the edge of a cliff in his old maroon Chevrolet Silverado. And it was Dante's mother who married a successful art dealer and moved to England.

But not before the "incident" which now resisted my efforts to forget: The "Cromley Incident", as Dante's mother referred to it forever after. Quite simply, I stole a Cromley and Finch silk necktie from the men's department at Bloomingdale's. Flamingo pink with yellow stripes. Awful to look at, but irresistibly goading me from the rack. Reach out. Pull it down. Walk away with it. But, before I could reach the exit, I saw the security guard approaching. So I stuffed the tie in Dante's pocket and left him to face the consequences. Not looking back. Except to push it away whenever the memory returned, as it just did, rejected, but not quite locked-up.

"Come with me, please," a voice thundered from the officer's desk, sparing me further memories.

As I walked over to the desk, another officer motioned me to follow him to the Custody Suite, making me feel that the seconds were already ticking, that time was being spent.

Two men, Dante and I, seated across the table from each other in a windowless interview room where souls were pushed one step further into hell. I was shocked by the prison uniform he was wearing: drab white and ill fitting. His handsome Mediterranean features were drawn, his thick black hair dishevelled and unwashed. The eyes, brown like the soil of his ancestors, heavy-lidded from lack of sleep. The lips, clues to his phenomenal appetite for women, tightly closed, as if pushing laughter out of his life. As for the muscular body (no taller than mine but broader, stronger), it seemed only a semblance of his former self.

"Not feeding you much, are they?" I said, hoping for a smile as we faced each other.

No smile. Not even that naughty one he used when he felt himself backed into a corner.

"Hey, Trev," he said. "What the bloody hell's going on?"

"I don't know, Dante. I assume it's related to the fact that Antonia is still missing."

"Of course it is. But in what way? What am *I* doing here? Why me?"

I leaned forward in the glaring neon and wiped the sweat off my upper lip, though the interview room was unnaturally cold.

"Look, Dante," I said. "Antonia has been missing –"

"Five days."

"Exactly."

"The police are looking for someone."

"And that someone is me?"

"I don't know, Dante," I mumbled, for the question had disturbed me, deeply, while stirring a sense of relief that it was him, not me, who was in custody.

"You don't know," he retorted. "But I'm the one in the clink. How come?"

"They've got the wrong man, obviously."

"Obviously. But someone's got to tell them it wasn't me. I'm not a heartless beast. I could never have done this."

"I believe you," I said, though my eyes were a little hasty in looking away.

"You bloody listen to me, Trev," he shouted and clutched my arm with trembling hands. "The police have got to catch the culprit and you've got to help them. The motherfucker who did this is out there somewhere and –"

"I will do all I can to find him."

I reached out, patted his shoulder and got up cutting the visit short.

"Keep up your spirits," I told him.

I walked away, not too quickly, at a pace becoming to a man who need not be hurried, a man quite capable of letting others enforce the rule of law. In other words, an innocent man.

THREE

June 18, 2005

When I arranged to meet with Honey Dew Saturday evening at 8, I didn't know that the police had recovered a body they had not yet identified.

I came home from the gallery at 6, in the pounding rain, and found two officers huddled under the maples on the sidewalk, an improbable shelter because of the youth of their leaves and the ferocity of the wind.

"Are you Trevor Snow."

Hardly a question, more of an accusation. Nevertheless, I nodded, with just a pause for breath, which was as near as I came to betraying the horrific discomfort their presence had inspired.

"Come in, come in," I urged them, fumbling with the key and opening up.

"Inspector Fielding and Sergeant Dale," one of them said, without specifying who was who. "We've been sent by our Serious Crime Directorate."

"I assumed as much."

"A few enquiries, sir."

Hatless and soaked myself, I led them into the library and offered them a sherry or something stronger.

"Don't drink while on duty," the taller of the two men said. He had a small narrow head and a long neck, much like that of a cobra.

"I'll take a beer," the other one said, no doubt accustomed to the flawed abstinence that I could smell on his breath as I poured a Beck's into a beer mug.

"Is it about my wife?" I asked, addressing the back of the tall officer as he ambled past me to position himself in front of the dead ashes in the fireplace.

But it was the plump one who answered. "Afraid so, sir."

Wait, I said to myself. *Don't say anything yet. Think before you talk.*

"Is she –?" I mumbled, in the voice of a man who knows nothing but fears everything.

"The body of a Caucasian female has been

found in Regent's Park Canal," the tall officer said. "Sergeant Dale will give you the details."

I had not expected to cringe as I did, but the stab of pain had caught me off guard. I looked away, tried to remain calm, as the sergeant coughed, cleared his throat and prepared to embark on the unsavoury task assigned to him by his superior.

"No positive identification has been made yet. However, we felt obliged to let you know," he said, mellowed by the drink and, perhaps, his own humanity.

"We tried to reach you several times," Inspector Fielding said. "But we were unable to find you."

"Sorry. I've been running around in circles."

At that precise moment I remembered my assignation with Honey Dew, outside the bar where she worked in Hampstead and, instinctively, I looked at my watch.

"Expecting anyone?" Inspector Fielding snapped, as he lowered himself into an armchair.

"My wife's father," I lied. "He's here from Italy and I thought that perhaps –"

"He has already been to see us," Sergeant Dale took out a small red notebook and began flipping through the pages. "Ah, here it is. Piero Giordano, father of the missing woman. Arrived day before yesterday from Naples, Italy, on Alitalia flight 163. Came down to the station this morning but failed to identify the body."

"Failed?" I echoed.

"Couldn't do it. Too upset. Collapsed on a chair, shaking his head, begging God for a miracle."

"So we left him alone," Inspector Fielding blurted. "Not up to us to question God's mercy." He paused before adding with a hideous smirk. "Or the devil's tricks for that matter."

I knew perfectly well he was waiting for my reaction. But I was too threatened, too anxious to be forthcoming. I stood in silence, until the inspector made the next move.

"You own an art gallery, don't you, Mr. Snow," he said.

"I'm one of two partners."

"But you make your own hours. You're not chained to a desk, are you?"

"I handle certain sales… in my own good time, yes."

"Which means your presence, or absence, needn't be conspicuous."

"Not sure what you mean."

"Your whereabouts might be difficult to trace."

"On the contrary, I have a straightforward routine, as I'm sure you know."

I said this, but I was thinking just the opposite. *Shrewd hound, the inspector; he takes the measure of his suspects and waits for them to trip.*

Sergeant Dale had gone back to his notes. "Hmm, where was I?"

"The body," Fielding prompted him.

"Ah, yes. The state of decomposition is rather advanced, I'm afraid, but… hmm… we need to attempt –"

From across the room Fielding interrupted his underling again. "Have you ever been in a morgue, Mr. Snow?" he asked, as if the question might mean something to me.

"No," I said.

"Cold place. The dead are cold. And so are some of the living." He paused and gave another of his stringent smiles before returning to his subject. "Tough thing to ask, but we need to identify the body on the mortuary slab."

Silence, as if none of us could dispel the marmoreal horror which awaited us.

"Mind if we go over the details?" This from Fielding, who no longer bothered to conceal the suspicion smouldering in his eyes.

"Go ahead," I said, meekly.

"It is assumed your wife was walking the dog in Regent's Park four days ago when she fell off York

Bridge into the water," Sergeant Dale said, reading from his notes.

"Or was pushed," Fielding interjected.

"Yes," Dale confirmed, and went on. "The current must have dragged her a couple hundred yards away from York Bridge. The body was found early this morning, tangled in the weeds, by an amateur photographer shooting a pair of swans and their cygnets. He was quite shaken. Ran all the way up to Albany Street to fetch a constable."

"Do you think –"

"Drowning," Fielding blurted. "That's what we think. Death by drowning. We haven't had the pathology report yet, but it appears that she went into the water alive."

My mouth felt chalk-dry. Like all men under intense scrutiny, I tried not to squirm under his watchful stare. "Are you telling me there is a suspicion of foul play?" I asked.

"It's only a hypothesis," Fielding replied, his eyes slipping away toward the handsome portrait above the mantelpiece. "Is this your wife?" he asked, still gazing at the stunning face that smiled, perhaps a trifle flirtatiously, from the wall.

"Yes," I said and I, too, stared at the enormous grass-green eyes, the elegant nose, the sensuous lips, the cascade of dark hair, glowing with gingery streaks.

"Beautiful woman," he said.

"Yes," I said. "She is very beautiful."

"A woman like that can push a man beyond rage."

Well, aren't you clever, I thought. But I said, "This is very difficult for me."

"For us, too, Mr. Snow. The snuffing of life is not one of the attractions of the profession," Fielding said, turning away from the portrait and addressing me with affected nonchalance, "You know how it is."

"I don't know much of anything any more… I know that my wife went out to walk the dog and…" A long agonized pause, then the question took shape in my mind and spilled, "What about the dog? Does anyone know what happened to him? He never came back, though he must have known his way home."

Sergeant Dale considered the query and seemed to wonder whether to address it or ignore it.

Fielding's voice cut through the pause. "The dog," he urged him, his patience dwindling fast.

Dale thumbed through his notes. "Ah, yes. Here it is on page 18," he said, picking his way through his notebook. "A fourteen-pound, brown and white, long-haired Jack Russell named, hmmm –"

"Cappuccino," I said.

"Like the coffee," the inspector translated for the convenience of his subordinate.

The sergeant nodded, appeared to make a mental note to engage an interpreter. "Right," he said. "Seems the little bugger has a limp."

"Yes," I said. "One of his legs is shorter than the others."

"Well, sir," Sergeant Dale concluded, tossing the last of his drink into his mouth. "They haven't found the dog yet."

Long silence. But Fielding's patience was not benign. He stood up, walked to the mantle, turned and stared at me across the room. "We've got a suspect," he announced.

That questioning look again, leaving me with an awkward dilemma. Should I pounce on the disclosure? Wait? Appear shocked? Marooned? Fielding obviously wanted some sort of drama.

"A suspect?" I echoed grimly.

"Yes."

"I suppose it's no good asking who."

"On the contrary," Fielding said, almost complacently. "It's someone you know."

"I know many people."

"Danilo Terranova."

"Dante!" I exclaimed. "That's impossible. He wouldn't –"

"At this time he's only a suspect."

"Why? In what way? What the hell could make you suspect him?"

"We received an anonymous phone call that points a finger in his direction."

I frowned and looked away, uneasily. "I didn't know the police took into account anonymous phone calls," I said.

"Oh, we do. Our experts on voice identification decide whether or not to reject them."

"I'll tell you one thing, Inspector. You are on the wrong track. Dante isn't the sort. He would never do this. He's a trusted friend, not a criminal."

"I didn't say *criminal*, Mr. Snow. I said *suspect*."

Suddenly I knew what was expected of me. I did not require any more prodding. I did not look at my watch again. I buried my face in my hands and ignored the flutter in my voice, each word struggling to make itself heard.

"Will you take me to the… the… Good Lord, I can't quite say it."

"The body," Inspector Fielding said, in the tone of a man for whom the word holds few surprises.

I did not reply, just nodded with enough emotion to suggest the viewing would be a prelude to a new onslaught of misery.

"Well then, let's go," the inspector said, and switched to a more focused bloodhound mode.

Sniff, growl, pursue. What next? Apprehend? Not likely. Seems all they have is circumstantial evidence. At this juncture anyway.

FOUR

June 17, 2005

The fruity connotation of Honey Dew's name sometimes pleased me and other times irritated me. But when I attempted to shorten it to Honey, on our very first assignation, almost two years ago, she said indignantly, "Your name *Trevor*. My name *Honey Dew*."

"What's wrong with Honey? All by itself?"

She knitted her small feathery eyebrows as if the question was not welcome, or not courteous, or not important. "Nothing wrong," she said, as she took off her tweed jacket, her scarf and her black stiletto sandals. "But not my name. My name Honey Dew Tung."

"Like the tree?"

"Yes. Chinese tree."

I knew already after those on-again, off-again

steamy sessions in a fourth-floor flat above a furniture store in Hampstead (which I had rented in an area not susceptible to the curiosity of neighbours) that, when challenged, this gorgeous little sex empress could display a blunt disdain, as stilted in annoyance as it was lavish in affection.

Now, observing that I seemed surprisingly unresponsive to her touch, she looked at me with a puzzled expression and asked, "What's wrong, Trevor?"

"This thing about my wife."

"I saw article in *Daily Mail*."

"You did? Today?"

"Didn't you?"

"No. Have you got a copy?"

"No. I saw newspaper at the tube station, on my way to work."

"You remember what it said?"

"Something about clues."

"What about them?"

"Clues lead to York Bridge, in Regent's Park, then gone," she said, her almond-shaped eyes wide open and a few strands of her coal-black hair waiting to be pushed back behind her ear.

"Photograph?"

"Yes. Big one. Pretty woman. Sad eyes. English people surprised when one person disappears. In my country thousands disappear. No one surprised."

Just then, the emptiness inside me, which felt like melancholy, turned into raw grief. Shaken, I put my head on Honey Dew's chest.

"Hug me," I said. "Please."

She did. She put her arms around me and drew me close to her, allowing me to be sheltered by her, yet alone in my sorrow.

"You're a nice girl, Honey Dew," I said, at last. "I'm lucky to have met you."

"You lucky I'm bad girl. I'm only nineteen, but I'm smart turning tricks. See what I mean?"

Proudly she contemplated the outcome of her labours, my prick finally stiffening under her expert fingers. But not for long. A sudden image of the front page of the *Daily Mail*, which I had been torn between reading and ignoring, withered my ardour.

"You really upset."

"Sorry, Honey Dew," I said, staring down at the blunt language of a reluctant cock.

But she drew breath and bent down again, her straight hair like a silk black curtain tickling my belly as her red valentine lips coaxed and stroked and salvaged the leftovers of my lust.

Trembling and aroused, I allowed myself to

submit to that adamant imperative, a stir of pleasure already tingling in my groin. Oblivion, I begged her. I want to forget. Him. Her. Myself. I want to tame the beast that pokes its head… ah, ah, ahhh… so that when my coital cries stopped and my weeping began they were one and the same, both hideous and exquisite.

Though I covered my face with my hands, I was unable to suppress certain images – her smile, his laughter, the touch of her hand, the look in his eyes when the two of them saw each other – images that turned my sobs into convulsive gasps like the rush at the heart of a waterfall.

Afterwards, gratified by the felicity of the outcome, we dressed and prepared to leave, she fixing her lipstick in the mirror, I taking the customary two hundred quid out of my wallet and leaving it on the night table.

"Do you do this for many men, Honey Dew?"

"Not many. Few."

"Would you do it for me if I didn't pay you?"

Her slanted eyes peered at me from under charcoal eyelids; then the scarlet lips, no longer smudged, broke into a smile.

"Of course," she said coyly. "But you rich man, I poor girl. Not equivalent."

"You mean fair."

"Right. Not fair, not square," she said, picking up the money and slipping it into the back pocket of her tight elegant jeans.

FIVE

June 16, 2005

I'll do anything, I thought, I'll go anywhere to avoid returning to the house where Piero Giordano, my wife's father, is sitting in the dark, chain-smoking and staring at the portrait of his vanished daughter. Is it possible to hide glaring guilt from his eyes? A bruised soul from his scrutiny?

I kept roaming in the murky twilight, asking myself at what point sadness turned into grief and grief into despair. Where did it lead? And to whom? Perhaps God (if I could invent Him) or repentance (if I knew how it felt) or absolution (if I could chastise myself enough).

Now, thinking of the occurrence from whose horror I had fled and from whose consequence I might never be able to extricate myself, I came upon the imposing medieval church across the road from Regent's Park – the Danish church I must have passed a thousand times without ever bothering to enter.

Thoughts of providence, of miracles, prompted me to push the massive wooden door. To my astonishment, it creaked open and let me in. A sense of Christian hospitality (perhaps Catholic since the church was named Saint Katharine) mingled with the overbearing smell of lit candles and incense.

How long since I was last in church? Too long to remember. Except for the image of Father Rowan, the crippled pastor of our Southern Baptist church in Florida, limping along the narrow aisle on his way to the altar. He had a walking stick which he used for support (as well as punishment). Dante and I loathed catechism, but had been warned by our parents that no church meant no dinner, no fishing, no movies.

Now, years later, inside this foreign church, the sound of my footsteps grew louder and louder as I walked across the nave, stopped before a crucified Christ, terrifying in his near-nakedness, his crown of thorns, his glazed eyes.

If it was true that He knew about the sins of the world and still forgave the multitudes, then He would understand the rage which had coursed through my blood, the anger which had seized and devoured me.

I bent down and bestowed a humble touch upon His lacerated feet. They were cool as marble, and so were the eyes that couldn't see. Or could they?

"I'm not looking for forgiveness, Lord. I just want to stop the sound of that splash."

I paused. I had barely expressed what I was there to say, and yet I was already spent. The rain seemed to have tapered off, and a bleak sun was shimmering on the stained glass windows as I tore myself away from the crucifix, my throat tight from swallowing the unshed tears, my footsteps hollow as my own faith.

SIX

June 16, 2005

My father-in-law, Piero Giordano, is a Caprese by birth, a fisherman by necessity and a father by miscalculation. Sometime in the spring of 1984, his young peasant common-law wife had misunderstood the rhythm method of contraception (as explained to her by the village priest), therefore creating life with one wrong monosyllable and giving birth to a stunningly beautiful baby girl they named Antonia.

But, overnight, the joyful event had turned tragic when the young mother paid the ultimate price for giving birth with only the village midwife to assist her during a difficult delivery.

Too preoccupied to dwell on the cruelty of fate, the anxious father, who until then had held a dignified but financially unrewarding position as a high school Italian teacher, had been forced to supplement his income by moonlighting as a fisherman. His frail rowboat (idle but for an occasional Sunday excursion) was dutifully sanded, painted, repaired and equipped with sturdy broad oars which would allow Piero to test the waters off the coast of Capri.

It had taken the village a few weeks to realize that Piero Giordano was in search of Someone to do Something about his meagre resources. But, having understood, the villagers (even the thriftiest) permitted themselves the luxury of charitable contributions.

Of course there was no one more deserving of help than the rugged, weather beaten, self-proclaimed fisherman, and no one better able to help him than the Almighty. Like all miracle-workers, the Almighty made Piero's fishnets heavy with flounder and sea bass and snappers, with bushels of calamari for good measure, thus enabling him to retain a certain amount of intellectual fantasy, while making life tolerable for his family.

But a tragic occurrence (the worst any parent can envision) had brought him to a foreign land. And yet, the more excruciating his sorrow, the more steadfast his faith.

Hearing the scratch of my key in the lock, he gave out a tremulous squeal of joy, "Antonia!"

"Sorry," I said. "It's me."

He appeared to have been waiting in the foyer; now, as he shuffled back into the library, his thin knobbly hands fumbled in his breast pocket in search of his cigarettes.

"*Scusi, ha una sigaretta?*"

"There's a pack of Marlboros on the desk."

"*Grazie, grazie.*"

Long minutes went by after his jerky efforts to light the cigarette; then the obvious question was asked, "Any news?"

"Not so far," I said.

"The *investigatore* was here."

"Who?"

"*Agente di polizia.* They put Missing Person signs all over London. I said to offer one thousand pounds reward. That's okay? You can pay?"

"Of course. I would have done the same if I could think straight."

"The *agente* said the sniffing dogs followed her smell to York Bridge, in Regent's Park." He paused and seemed to struggle with a language he was not comfortable with. "What was Antonia doing at York Bridge? *Voglio dire*, why did she go there?"

"It's one of her favourite walks. More so after she

got the dog."

I stirred the logs in the fireplace and felt their heat on my cheeks, my neck. Steaming hot and surprisingly disagreeable. The crackling noises were unable to drown out Piero's footsteps pacing back and forth, followed by his heavily accented words.

"The *agente* asked if Antonia is depressed."

"I wonder how they would know that."

"Know? She *is* depressed?"

"Yes."

He looked startled by the information, which might imply his own failure as an intuitive parent.

"I had no idea," he mumbled, through a cloud of smoke.

"Nothing dreadful," I said. "More like the blues. Or a locked-up sadness she's been unable to express."

He nodded, dropping ashes in the fireplace, then asked through another cloud of smoke, "You have marriage problems?"

I felt myself blush and quickly turned away, leafing through the bundle of letters, bills, gallery accounts, that were piled up on the desk.

"We do," I said, at last. "But no more than any other couple."

"The *agente* thinks Antonia has a lover. That is true?"

I slammed my fist on the desk and turned to him a face both outraged and distraught.

"Those bastards," I said. "How dare they accuse her of infidelity?"

Startled by my outburst, he hastened to offer an explanation. "The *agente* said a jealous husband, *un cornuto*, feels a sudden hurt. *Mi perdoni*, Trevor," he added miserably. "That's what he said."

I felt immensely sorry for him – mostly because he was unaware of the depths of sorrow he might be destined to experience. I wished I could play straight with him, or, at least, that I could stamp out the fear in his eyes.

"The *agente* wants to talk with you," he said quietly.

"They already have. But I'll talk to them again and again. As long as necessary."

"With Dante, too."

"He's a good friend. He'll do whatever he can to help."

"He came this afternoon."

"Did he?" I said, feigning surprise.

"Brought a bottle of *Montepulciano*. To calm the nerves. Want some? A glass of red wine is not going to hurt while we wait."

Till when? I wondered, as I uncorked the bottle and poured two large goblets. For him there was no harm in waiting. He enjoyed the protection of his ignorance, which justified his hope, his optimism. Unlike my own devastation, which left me unanchored, a man with a future as murky as his past.

"Antonia wrote me a letter a month ago," he said, gulping down his wine. "*Lo stavo leggendo* when you came in. Want to hear the funny part? I translate for you.

"Please."

He put on his reading glasses and scanned the letter for the morsel that might amuse me.

"So, you see, Papa," he recited, "the English people think that all we do is eat and drink and get fat. Which makes me laugh so much when they see that I'm tall as a pine tree and skinny as…"

He interrupted himself, searching for a word. "Hmm… What you call, in the fields, what frightens birds?"

"Scarecrow."

"…and skinny as a scarecrow."

He folded the letter and returned it to his breast pocket.

"Thanks, Piero," I said, relieved that there appeared to be no mention of quarrels, of anger, of guilt, of wounding and being wounded.

The wine was beginning to soothe my nerves. I

no longer felt threatened, on the brink of just enough misery to spill a burst of *mea culpa* into our dialogue. I swirled the last of the wine in my goblet, inching toward a lighter mood.

"I need to change my clothes and tidy up a bit," I told him. "I don't think I've looked in the mirror since –"

"I understand," he said, and smiled his Antonia smile, bright and disturbingly haunting.

"Then we can go out and have supper somewhere. What do you think?"

He didn't respond for a long time. When at last he did, he spoke hesitantly, as if afraid he might say more than he had intended.

"I'm just a foolish man, sometimes. And I don't have… how you say, things with value. Except my daughter and my faith." He paused, and added humbly, "*Molto bella la fede*, Trevor. So I go and pray now. I pray that Antonia comes home soon."

SEVEN

June 16, 2005

I rushed out of my home as if I were leaving a spook house. Couldn't get away fast enough. But outside the headlines were vociferous.

REGENT'S PARK MYSTERY: SUICIDE OR MURDER? MISSING LOCAL RESIDENT LAST SEEN IN PARK. FEW CLUES IN WOMAN'S DISAP-PEARANCE. TRAIL DEAD ENDS AT BRIDGE.

However fast I walked the headlines followed. High street, low street, back street, side street, fuck-you-all street. I kept my head bent and my eyes down, a *j'accuse* glaring at me from every photo-graph, article, description, assumption.

But it was not difficult to escape the newspaper-hawkers. It meant drifting into Regent's Park, forest-green and fluttery, the sunshine reflected on the puddles after the rain had stopped.

I had not prepared myself for the shock.

He was the last person I expected I would see standing a few feet away, leaning against the rail atop the parapet of York Bridge, gazing at the water as the sun went down. What the hell did he expect to find there?

"Hello, Dante."

Though he turned away when he saw me, he did not seem surprised that I had materialized and was standing beside him. Tired, dishevelled, there seemed to be a mixture of fury and frustration about him, his longish dark hair tangled, untidy, his eyes both feverish and elusive. For once, his ever present camera was not slung over his shoulder. I was sickened that such distress could not be shared, that the candour of our lifelong friendship had to be scraped, like a tumour, out of existence.

"Doesn't make sense," Dante said, searching the water, which tonight resembled a marshy creek. "I don't believe she jumped."

I nodded and peered down at the stream, a man-made waterway that got filled with water from the mainland. I had read somewhere that the depth of this narrow channel was just over two metres and that the bottom was made of puddle clay, hard as concrete. At this juncture the water

was moving rapidly, trailing wisps of debris –
leaves, feathers, twigs, the odd plastic bag.

"The police think she may have just wandered
off," I said. "Amnesia, or something."

The silver maples, budding above his head, flut-
tered and dropped two reddish florets onto his
hand. He stared at them and in a touchingly awkward gesture slipped them into the pocket of his
jacket.

"Did she ever tell you..." he began, at last
raising his head to look at me, "...that someone
might be stalking her?"

"Why would anyone be after her?"

"A homeless guy, a lunatic, a pervert."

"The dog would have found his way home,
wouldn't he?"

"Yeah... shit, Trev, I don't know."

"I'm not saying it's impossible, Dante, but I
doubt it. This is London, not Rwanda. It doesn't
make sense, even if you look at it from all unex-
pected angles, except –"

"Except what?"

"Depression."

I saw in his face a look of uneasiness, as if he
were about to shoulder an awful burden. "Antonia
didn't seem her cheerful self lately, did she?" he
acknowledged wearily.

"Not at all."

"She was depressed. That's your explanation?"

"Her behaviour was weird."

"In what way?"

"She had lost weight. Seemed restless. Exhausted at night, not interested in sex. I got the feeling, whenever she left the house, that she might not come back."

"God! Moody I can understand. But depressed? That's serious, isn't it?"

I did not agree or disagree. I waited for him to sort out his thoughts and wrestle with his conscience.

"You think she... she just wandered off?" he asked.

"Don't know what to think, Dante. I'm trying to persuade myself that there is a logic to all this. Sometimes irrational behaviour has a logic of its own."

But he refused to be mollified by an abstract morsel of philosophy and bluntly said, "I got a call from an Inspector Freeman, or Felman, or –"

"Fielding," I told him.

"Anything to do with your visit yesterday to the police station?"

"Probably."

"Well, this guy thinks he's a bloody genius. But he hasn't found her, has he?"

"Obviously not."

"What about you? What are *you* doing to find her?"

"A lot more than showing up at this bridge and asking dumb questions. I've been to interviews with the police, the investigators, anyone who may –"

At that moment the pair of swans appeared, haughty and magnificent, gliding next to each other to remind me of a tableau which had already been staged, performed. But not all the details were the same. Tonight there was no moon, only a silvery flicker behind the thickening clouds. And the water was grey, for the so-called blue-green algae which had struck certain streams seemed to have cleared. Now the swans were slashing the water outwards into broadening ripples as they displayed their arrogant heads.

"That stinking slush is gone," Dante said, pointing at the water. Then, ignoring our angry exchange, he asked, "What do you think happened to Antonia?"

I put both my hands on the railing and struggled to hold my rage captive. Unseen. Unheard. And yet I was just as disturbed to feel my fury beginning to subside. I was never more lucid than when confronted with rage. Unlike others, who became erratic and confused, rage made me aware of the imperatives, prevented me from backing off.

"I think she left," I said.

"Without saying good-bye?"

"Walking out speaks volumes, don't you think?"

"Not in her case. She's clearheaded and sensible. Never struck me as irresponsible."

"She has been unhappy for a long time."

"Didn't leave a note, didn't take a goddamn thing –"

"She took the dog."

He nodded, visibly upset. Antonia's walking out and taking the dog with her presented him with an equation he was unable to explain.

"Piero's alone at the house, I said. "I'd better get back."

"I saw Piero this afternoon. Took him a bottle of wine. *Montepulciano*, one of his favourites."

"You remember that?"

"From our days in Capri, when we first met him. How could I forget?"

I had not forgotten either. But it seemed so far away, as if it had happened in another lifetime.

"I was sorry to see Piero so unhappy," Dante said. "Felt I had nothing to give him. No hope. Not even a bloody lie. In another hour it will be midnight Italian time. He's an old man. He can defend himself by falling asleep. One way to forget, isn't it?"

EIGHT

June 15, 2005

I huddled under my umbrella and contemplated the Thames, sombre and grey in the pelting rain. Dante, drenched and disdainful of the elements, kept walking next to me until we reached Albany Street Police Station, across Regent's Park, and offered to go in with me.

"Don't bother," I told him. "I'll manage on my own."

I dreaded a meeting which would prompt intense questioning from the police but had been unable to convince Dante we should wait before reporting Antonia missing.

"Can't stand it any more," he had yelled, and pleaded with me to contact the police.

This oasis of the unknown was housed on a third floor unit of the Police Station, littered with files, newspapers, telephones, bulging briefcases, photographs, and coffee mugs.

Ian McAndrews, the detective in charge of the Missing Persons Unit, was standing behind his desk, gazing out of a window that overlooked charcoal rooftops where jittery pigeons were shaking the rain off their feathers. He was a heavy, short man with gold-rimmed spectacles, a thick reddish moustache and reddish tufts bristling out of his nostrils.

"Dismal day," he growled, as he shook my hand and we sat down across from each other. "Sorry to drag you out, but it would have been difficult to discuss this over the phone."

"Thanks for agreeing to see me."

"Sounds urgent. Lady vanishes into thin air, she might be held up at gunpoint by a couple of thugs."

I remained silent as McAndrews adjusted his spectacles, which were sliding down his nose.

"It's been... how long since your wife went out to walk the dog in the park?"

"Twenty-two hours."

"What took you so long to report this?"

"Didn't think of her as *missing*. Assumed she wanted time on her own. Blamed it on her temperament."

"Which is?"

"Italian. Volatile. A bit despondent lately."

His head lifted from taking notes and he frowned.

"Despondent?" he echoed.

"Depressed."

"Is she seeing a psychiatrist?"

I shook my head. "My wife comes from a small village in Italy, Detective –"

"McAndrews."

"They treat depression with mud baths, herbal teas, mushrooms –"

"Not toadstools, I hope."

The questioning proceeded smoothly and predictably, aimed at gathering information that might prove useful without making me uncomfortable. On it flowed, from one detail to another, as McAndrews focused on harvesting information that might turn a blur into a woman.

"Height?" he asked, the scratch of his fountain pen mingling with the steady patter of rain.

"Five foot eight."

"Weight?"

"125 pounds, more or less."

"Hair?"

"Dark brown, with gingery streaks."

"Eyes?"

"Jade green."

"*What* kind of green?"

"Her eyes change with the light, from grass-green to jade."

He raised his eyebrows, as if he found the information improbable, but moved on to the next question.

"How long have you been married?"

"Almost six months."

"Newlyweds!"

"Practically, yes."

"Though it's all relative, isn't it? If you're unhappy, six months is too long."

"We're very happy."

"Until this... hmm, unfortunate occurrence." He paused, briefly, then resumed the questioning in his kindly voice. "Is it unusual for your wife to walk the dog at that time?"

"No. She walked him every evening around six."

"While you are still at work?"

"I usually leave the gallery at seven."

"Normal routine, I see. Can you think of anything that breaks the mould?"

"No."

An hour later Detective McAndrews fired what appeared to be his concluding questions. "You don't have any *theories*, do you, Mr. Snow, as to who might be involved in this disappearance?"

"I can't come up with anything tangible. It's as if my brain is switched off."

"No theories, then," he said in a sympathetic voice. As he put aside the form and flopped back into his swivel armchair, he added, "Suppose you were me. How would you proceed with this investigation? What would be your best lead?"

I gazed at him for some time, letting him know that I understood he was probing the wound, that I didn't object, that I could tolerate anything but stagnation, that I had one purpose in mind and one only: to find my missing wife.

"I'm glad I'm not you," I said in a choked voice. "It's difficult enough being myself. All I can do is wind the clock backwards and stop it at the precise moment when –" No longer able to keep my composure, I buried my head in my hands and remained silent.

My outburst got through to him, for the next moment he was escorting me to the door, patting my back and saying, "Don't give up, Mr. Snow. We'll do whatever we can to find your wife for you."

Outside the office door, I stopped in my tracks as a black cat with sulphur-yellow eyes dashed in front of me from the hallway and disappeared through an open door.

"Anything wrong?" the detective asked.

"That black cat," I gasped. "It came out of no-where."

"Oh, that's Henry, our mascot. He survived a horrific fire in Chelsea. No one claimed him, so we adopted him." He waited, surprised that I didn't move, utterly still, frozen. "Not superstitious, are you?"

"Very much so," I said, managing to make it sound as if all of mankind was afflicted with quirks through no fault of its own. "Is there any other way out?"

"I'm afraid not," the detective said, affably. "But you needn't worry. There's a smudge of white on Henry's chest. So he's not all black."

I felt him watching me as I made my way down-stairs and paused before the uniformed policeman who stood by the entrance. Was Detective McAndrews pondering the facts he had gathered? Or those he hadn't?

NINE

June 15, 2005

I dreamed of being an artist all my life. But I also knew, instinctively, that my expectations would exceed my meagre efforts. Such awareness left me with no choice but to snuff my dreams and move on.

An interesting break came two years ago in the form of H. H. Tompkinson, the art gallery owner who had married Dante's mother and pinned his hopes of happiness on her. It had worked well for them, until her recent death of septicaemia (she had stepped on a rusty nail in their farm in Surrey). He and Josephine (his daughter from a previous marriage) invited me to lunch at *Claridge's*, for the purpose of "discussing business".

We were sitting at a front corner table near the window, and they had just fetched our drinks.

"Am I right in thinking that you're looking for a new job?" Tompkinson asked, gulping down his martini and signalling the waiter for another.

"Yes," I said, fully aware that Dante had spilled the news that I was out on the streets with my begging bowl.

Josephine took a sip of her lager and a puff from her thin Cuban cigar. "Why did you leave the Langbourne Gallery?" she asked, running her fingers through her bristly, coppery red, short hair.

"The owner and I were at odds with one another," I said, in a voice meant to discourage further inquiries.

But Josephine insisted. "At odds?" she said, puffing away. "In Art? In marketing?"

"In ideology," I told her.

"Can you elaborate?"

"I made no secret of my passion for contemporary art, regardless of its potential. My employer was far more interested in salesmanship."

"Not much good dealing with geniuses if they don't sell," Josephine said.

"It's worth a try," I told her. "Since we couldn't agree, I left."

"Quite right," Tompkinson agreed. "If you have lost the battle, withdraw your cavalry. And move on."

Josephine raised her eyebrows, but she did not contradict her father, who was now, three martinis later, offering to make me a partner in his gallery.

"Your association with our gallery will suit your independent streak," he said. "Come around in the morning. We'll discuss it."

"What about Dante?" I asked. "Wouldn't he want this opportunity for himself?"

Josephine laughed uproariously, as if the same futile question had been asked many times.

"Dante's not interested in the gallery," Tompkinson said. "At least for now, while I'm still paying for his meals."

"He's having fun with his Nikon D80," Josephine volunteered. "Imitating the *paparazzi*."

"So, it's up to you," Tompkinson concluded, and got up.

As I thanked him and got ready to leave, Josephine took one last puff from her cigar. "You a married man, cherub?" she asked.

"Not yet," I said.

"Perennial bachelor? Like Dante?"

"No. I expect to fall in love and marry –"

"And live happily ever after," Josephine cut me off, pulling out a chain watch from the waistband of her trousers. "I must run, but I look forward to your… how did Father put it?"

"Moving on," I said quietly, out of earshot of her drunk father.

* * *

That had been then. Now, after what seemed to me far too slow a stream of traffic from Regent's Park to Albemarle Street, I parked the Jaguar in my usual spot and walked over to the Albemarle Gallery. I stood a moment at the window, contemplating the large, brightly-coloured IN SEARCH OF A DREAM, painted by our pride and joy (and chief money-maker), Peregrine Heathcote. The work, oil in canvas, exploited his fascination with colour – blue, gold and red – and teased the viewer into thinking they, too, might be able to "see" what the girl was looking at through her binoculars.

Such a disquieting thought brought me back to my own nightmare. Should I turn around? But to go where? My distress was the same wherever I was.

"We sold FLIGHT OF FANCY," Josephine said, as I walked in. "The American chap was here again. Left a fat check as a deposit."

"Anything else?" I asked.

She gave me a strange look which voiced her disapproval.

"Haven't got art in the brain, have you?" she said.

"I have many worries, Josephine. The gallery is just one of them."

"I suppose you're worried about the lease."

I had forgotten we were in the process of renegotiating the lease.

"Well, you needn't worry," Josephine said. "My father's solicitor is already dealing with it."

"Good," I said.

As I moved away toward my office at the back of the gallery, she handed me a bundle of mail.

"Your friend the lothario telephoned twice," she said.

"Dante? What did he say?"

"Wanted to know where Antonia was."

"At the house."

"He said she wasn't there."

The words frightened me, confirmed the nightmare. Josephine sensed a disturbance and narrowed her eyes, watery blue and inquisitive, under the mop of red bristles.

"Anything wrong?" she asked.

After looking for an answer and finding none, I was rescued by the noisy shuffle of footsteps on the entrance, which announced Dante's arrival.

"Where the hell is Antonia?" he stormed. "She missed a lecture at the Fine Arts."

"What lecture?" I asked, sounding surprised.

"Fauvism. Given by a curator from The Hermitage."

"My apologies," I said. "I'm sure she'll catch the next one."

"Not unless she goes to St Petersburg."

Josephine gave a sardonic grin and addressed Dante. "Didn't know you were interested in art."

"Didn't you?" he said, and turned to her. "One wonders where the ever-curious Miss Tompkinson gets her information."

"Tarot cards," Josephine purred.

I was too preoccupied to join in the conversation. "Come into my office," I said to Dante. "There's something I want to discuss with you."

Under Josephine's reptilian stare, we disappeared into the room at the back of the gallery. I could feel my heart thumping inside my chest.

"What is it?" Dante asked, as I closed the door.

"Antonia," I said.

"What about her?"

"She's left."

"Left?"

"She went out to walk the dog and didn't come back."

"When?"

"Last night."

"Last *night*!" he shouted.

Through his astonishment, I could detect a glimmer of excitement which was not difficult to interpret. *Thus has she spoken, and thus has her husband understood.* In other words, my loss, his gain.

"What have you done about it?" he asked.

"Nothing."

"Why the hell not?"

"What is there to do?"

"Call the police. Report a missing person."

"I don't think she's missing, Dante. I think she's left. I don't want to embarrass her – or myself – by getting her name involved with the police."

But he was not convinced. Most unusual, was the assumption I read in his frown, his startled eyes, his white-lipped rigidity.

"People don't just walk out," he said. "Unless they're weird or irrational. Antonia is neither."

"I understand your point. What I'm trying to tell you is that you don't always need a reason. She may have left because it was the only thing to do."

The silence lasted a very long time. Just as he had accepted my explanation and harboured a pathetic hope that she might have chosen him over me, did he now shudder to think that she might have walked away from us both? In his anxiety, he stomped heavily up and down my office, the floorboards wailing under the abuse.

"Christ!" he yelled. "Where do you think she went?"

"Back to Italy," I told him.

"Have you called Piero?"

"Not yet."

"Call him now, Trev. Him and the police. You would never forgive yourself if something happened to her and you had done nothing about it."

I nodded, feeling that I had caught his apprehension. For an awful moment, as I scrambled for a list of phone numbers on the rolodex, I wondered if I would be able to find my voice.

"Here's the number," Dante said, stepping aside gingerly as I approached.

It occurred to me with amazement that I was moving with apparent ease, that I felt neither terror nor shame, only a vague sorrow, and a bit of revulsion, like dregs of vomit left in my throat.

TEN

June 14, 2005

Once, long ago (must have been in the early eighties), Dante and I were fishing on Flagler Drive. We always chose our side of the bridge that established the boundaries between those of us, the working middle class in West Palm Beach, and them, the ultra-elite socialites along South Ocean Boulevard. At one point we watched a seagull plunge into Lake Worth and re-emerge with a large silver fish twisting and flapping as it was about to be devoured.

"Hey, did you see that?" Dante asked.

"Yes," I said. "Disgusting."

"How is he different from us?"

"The seagull?"

"Same thing. Only for him it's food, for us it's fun," he fumed, as he packed up his bait, hooks, line and pole and walked away. Which may have defined him as a bit of an idealist (at least to himself), while possibly sparing the life of a catfish.

I hadn't thought about that incident for quite some time. But it flashed through my mind tonight as I walked faster and faster, away from York Bridge.

Rushing, on the pathway across the lawns, I stumbled on the root of an ancient horse-chestnut and hit the ground with a thud and a pleasurable sensation which I identified as pain. So I could feel again. A palpable discomfort in my elbows and knees had replaced the sense of nothingness I had accepted as the erosion caused by despair. The fall had ripped the fabric of my trousers and bruised my knee. The pain had come spontaneously, jolting me like someone just roused from sleep. A squirrel darted past, frightened by the mound of living flesh on his path. Somewhere in the foliage above me an owl hooted.

Come on, you bastard, I said to myself. *Too late for regret. Too early for remorse. The deed is done. Accept it for what it is. A taste of your own destiny. Unchanged and unchangeable.*

But though I attempted to get up, I was anchored to the mud, shaking, wiping off a slimy and repulsive filament of vomit which hung from my lips.

And still the tears wouldn't come. Perhaps later,

when I walked into the empty house. When I dragged myself upstairs and saw her rosary lying on the dresser. When I crawled into bed and found her pink silk nightgown folded under her pillow. When the telephone began to ring. When questions without answers cast a shadow on my path.

But the human brain is tough. Ingenious in its capacity to camouflage guilt. And quite resilient. Someday, I predicted to myself, I will no longer focus on *that* moment, I will no longer think *that* grinding thought, because everything, even despair, will have eroded with the passing of time.

ELEVEN

June 14, 2005

I poked my head out of the library into the foyer and saw that Antonia was wearing a white cotton T-shirt and a skirt whose green was that of grasshoppers. She was putting on her windbreaker and trying to clip the dog's leash onto his collar – a difficult task since he was yelping and whimpering and leaping onto the elegant recamier (just re-covered in French brocade) at the far end of the foyer. Damn! His scratching at the furniture drove me to dementia, though it seemed to leave Antonia unconcerned.

"Have you seen my keys?" she asked.

"Next to your wallet, on the kitchen table," I told her. "Where are you going?"

"Taking Cappuccino for a walk in the park."

"Wait for me. I'll come along."

Would I have been surprised if she had said, *No, I'd rather be alone.* Perhaps. But it might have changed the course of our lives.

"*Vengo subito,*" I told her, using a recently learned expression from my Italian Phrase Book for Travellers.

Outdoors the evening was clear, crisp. Lilacs, both lavender and white, were blooming along fences with perfumed exuberance. We walked across the road and entered Regent's Park, a bit emptier than you would expect on such a magnificent summer night.

"Antonia," I said. "We need to talk, don't we?"

"Yes," she agreed, in a touching voice, a voice that assumed I knew, as she did, that something was terribly wrong between us.

"I don't know how it happened," I began, tentatively. "But it's not what it used to be, is it?"

"Things change, Trevor."

"In what way?"

"Love is tricky. For some it grows, for others…" She paused and struggled to find a word less cryptic but, perhaps, crueller than the first. "…it crumbles."

And yet, even as I heard the words, I wished myself inside her crumbling love. To repair it. To strengthen it. To rekindle the illusion. In the unhappy silence that followed, I took a breath and blurted the question, "Is it because of him?"

"No," she said. "Nothing to do with him."

No need to identify *him*. In the walled garden of our dead love, there was only one bit of wild scrub growing between us. *Him*. Whenever I thought we had left him behind, he poked his head up, stronger than before.

"I don't believe you," I said. "I think you fell in love with Dante, but married me instead."

"Why would I do that?"

"Because I'm the one who went after you while he… he was unpredictable. You weren't sure how he felt toward you."

"It's not that simple," she said, without looking at me.

We were in the gardens now, flanked by rose-bushes on either side of the path, some bursting with colour, others already wilting in the early days of summer.

"Besides," I said, "you knew that if you married me, you could have him, too."

She stopped, suddenly, and fixed her startled eyes on my face. "Wrong," she said. "I married you for love. *Per amore, si capisce*. But your love for me is too intense. It suffocates me. Love shouldn't be a prison."

But she was wrong about that. Love *is* a prison. Indifference sets you free.

We walked on in silence, passing a few people along the way. A distance runner from Kenya (as announced on his sweatshirt). A white-haired nurse pushing a pram. Two pretty girls in uniforms. A tramp in mud-spattered Wellingtons.

"I think we should spend a little time away from each other," Antonia said.

"What do you mean?"

"I should go to Anacapri. Visit my father. Give us both time to reflect."

The path sloped gently downhill toward the stream, sprinkled with reddish florets from the silver maples. The florets lay scattered on the surface of the water, neither floating nor sinking, just swirling around the roots of the weeping willows beyond which a row of houseboats was tucked back into the reeds.

"The water looks dirty," Antonia said.

"Because of the algae," I said, as we kept walking in a mauve sunset that was quickly giving way to darkness.

At one point Antonia bent down and unclipped the dog's leash from his collar. Joyously, he limped ahead on the path, only to crouch and deposit several foul-smelling, rust-brown pellets, followed by a frantic scratching of the concrete with his hind legs. The abrasive sound mortified me, intensified my fierce distaste.

"I don't want you to go," I said. "I don't want you to leave me."

She placed her hand on my arm, and that simple gesture, the finality of it, the knowledge that worse would follow, scorched my throat and made me blink off the unwanted tears.

"Please, Antonia," I begged her. "Don't run away from me."

"Anacapri is not running away. It's home."

We had reached York Bridge and she stopped and leaned against the railing to look at the water. Smaller than a river, larger than a stream, flowing faster than usual, the water-line quite high, almost topping the banks.

"If you go, you'll never come back," I said.

The sunset had turned into evening, with a nearly full moon pitched very high, brighter now that the clouds had parted. It was a cold winter moon, neither silver nor mercury, but rather bone-white, slowly emerging from the clouds.

"Of course I'll come back," Antonia said.

There was a ripple in the water, caused by a large swan gliding toward the promise of bread-crumbs. Another swan, its mate, was half-hidden by the sagging branches of a large weeping willow, its trunk bearing an ancient pattern of nicks and cuts.

"Let's not talk about it any more," Antonia said, and pointed at the water. "What beautiful swans!"

At that moment the dog stood on his hind legs and clumsily pawed at my knees, scraping and scratching the fine wool gabardine with his muddy claws.

"Get off me! Damn it!" I shouted, but he ignored my command.

"Down, Cappuccino," Antonia said. "Down."

Too late. I had already picked him up with one hand and, moving with stunning swiftness, I tossed him over the railing into the water.

Antonia's enormous eyes were fixed upon me in the moonlight. Beautiful eyes, greener than grass. Eyes that broke the heart of the men who looked into them.

"You bastard!" she said.

"I'm sorry, I –"

She wasted no time. As swiftly as I had moved, she stepped out of her shoes and climbed onto the parapet and over the railing.

There was a tense pause as she clutched the railing and looked down, dangling a moment, before she let go and fell the short distance onto the mound of soil and scruffy grasses on the bank. Clambering to her feet, she lifted her head as if to cast one last look at where I stood above her.

Then she jumped into the water.

The splash was urgent, huge.

Her long hair came undone and floated behind her as she swam toward the dog with strokes that were encumbered by brush and debris. The dog had heard her approaching and now changed the course of his frantic paddling toward her.

She reached him almost immediately and, still swimming awkwardly with one arm, held him tightly with the other and headed back toward the bank.

But then he slipped out of her grasp and disappeared under a clump of wild grasses or reeds, or whatever wilderness polluted the water.

Antonia dove under, again and again.

I watched her slender body, now weighed by her soaked clothes, lifting itself up to survey the surface, then plunging down under the coarse vegetation.

"Cappuccino," she called, whenever she surfaced. "*Vieni qui.*"

In the moonlight I could see the sludgy grasses in the water, their slender stems, and wondered how anyone could pluck anything from that muck.

"Trevor," she called. "Help!"

The fear I had felt when I heard the splash now spread to my arms and legs. I bent down and began to untie my shoelaces with shaky fingers.

"Trevor," she cried. "The current!"

I sprang forward to the railing and saw that she had begun to drift away. I forced my legs to move, to get ready to leap over the parapet. And stopped. Love and rage battled within me with equally intense ferocity.

Antonia went under.

There were ripples as she re-emerged, covered in slime, and managed to grab onto a low willow branch, which shuddered under the strain, causing some egrets to fly away, shrieking. The branch snapped and broke off as Antonia sank and re-emerged again.

"Trevor," she called, in a muffled voice, desperately paddling, drifting away.

A wave of love shook my body and washed over my skin, my sweat, my pores. But not for long. A grim certainty flashed through my mind.

When Antonia opened her mouth again, no words reached my ears.

The only sound was the unstoppable flow of the stream.

Then the moon was eclipsed.

Without its silver glow, I was plunged into darkness, tormented by thoughts that seemed to tumble forth.

Go to her.

No, don't.

She's drifting away.

Let her go.

There's still time.

No. It's over. There's nothing left to salvage.

Then what are you waiting for?

Don't know.

Run, you fool.

Where to?

Who cares? Get out!

I grabbed the leash and threw it over the railing. I picked up her shoes, stroked them, held them against my face. Then I threw them into the water.

Fighting the panic which had taken hold of me, I began to walk away from the bridge, onto the path, and almost collided with a cyclist.

"Watch where you're going, you fucking idiot," he yelled as he zipped by.

He didn't know, did he, that there are worse indignities, for a desperate man, than being called an idiot.

TWELVE

June 11, 2005

I met Dante outside *Claridge's,* where he had been photographing the *Cartier* jewellery show on assignment for *Vogue.*

"Great rocks in there," he said, the camera slung over his shoulder. "Have to get back in an hour. They're expecting some gorgeous birds. Want to come?"

He did not mean of the feathered variety, and I had no desire to join him.

"No," I said. "It's after ten. I should go over to the gallery."

"Really, Trev. Don't you ever get tired of being faithful?"

"Absolutely not."

He gave an indulgent laugh as we walked on in the glorious sunshine, leaving Bond Street behind and making our way across Grosvenor Square, with its quaint fountains and majestic oaks.

"Let's get some coffee," Dante said, as we plunged into the bustle of Oxford Street.

But he stopped in his tracks to photograph a street violinist, playing to a crowd that didn't listen, just rushed by through the vertigoes of indifference.

"Keep playing, mate," Dante told him. "Your music goes straight to the balls."

Which made the fellow grin and produce another wave of magical sounds.

"You like taking photographs, don't you?"

"Things look different through the lens," Dante said. "Sharper. More exact."

"Not always. Sometimes the lens distorts the image."

"Rarely. As you know, I'll photograph anything on this planet, except –"

A fire. The one photograph he would never take. Though he rarely spoke of it, his experience had left him scarred.

"Anyway," I said. "I find it curious that if the lens distorts the image, it's art. If life does, it's deception."

"What are you trying to say?"

"That I'm unhappy about the rumours being spread by your stepsister, Josephine."

"That hag. How would she know anything about me? A man would turn into a *castrato* rather than screw her."

"She thinks you're having an affair with Antonia."

This was not the first time that Antonia had come between us. The rivalry had started from the moment we met her. But Dante's deception had never been so cunning. He swallowed his discomfort and found the logical explanation to dispel the rumour.

"It's Josephine's penis envy," he said.

"So you're *not* having an affair with Antonia."

"Of course not," he said, in a voice that established he would deny it and go on denying it no matter what evidence was used against him.

But he looked away as he smoothed back his hair and walked on.

It was more than I could bear. I stopped and stared at Dante's back. But, even in his turmoil, he realised I wasn't keeping up, and turned around.

"Now what?" he asked.

"Let me spell it out," I said. "You've never been above poaching my girls. Sue in high school. Mimi on the Paris vacation. Marianne at the –"

"What the fuck are you talking about? I *gave* you Antonia."

"Aw, come on, Dante. That's delusional."

Our quarrels had always had a pattern. He argued, and I argued, both as persuasive (or belligerent) as possible. Until Dante lost his Latin temper and became suddenly angry, despondent, sullen or whatever the occasion called for.

He gave an impatient toss of his head and shouted, "Accusing me of betrayal? Is that what you're doing?"

"No," I said lamely. "I'm only saying that if I'm sporting horns bigger than a mountain goat, I want to know about it."

"Oh, nice analogy. Brilliant!" he fumed, and hailed a passing taxi.

"What you don't understand –" I began, as I prepared to follow Dante into the taxi.

But he slammed the door leaving me stranded on the sidewalk.

* * *

I found Antonia in the kitchen, where she was baking fresh figs stuffed with mascarpone cheese, from her Aunt Flaminia's recipe.

"Please cancel our dinner with Dante tonight," I asked her and paddled through my own gloom toward the library, where the dog had found my sunglasses and was chewing them like a captured bone.

"Drop it!" I yelled, and saw that Antonia had followed me into the library.

"I know about the quarrel," she said. "Dante called and apologised for not offering you a lift."

"Did he tell you what the *quarrel* was about?"

"The usual stuff, he said."

"He's an expert at deluding everyone around him."

"Deluding?"

"Deceiving, beguiling, whatever."

I pushed away the dog, who had leaped onto the leather armchair. I wiped my glasses with elaborate care and sat down.

"Dante asked me to remind you that old friends should be forgiving," Antonia said.

"Oh! So now he's preaching. Why should I… Hey, Antonia! I think your figs are burning!"

She took off with a squeal and nothing more was said.

But that evening, at Dante's flat, over *capellini primavera* and a *Trentino di San Leonardo* from Dante's wine cellar, we had become a foursome. The lady he introduced had hot pink hair and sublime breasts. She looked quite comfortable in skin-tight pants and a sequinned T-shirt of shimmery purple and pink. Such attributes were in contrast with a curious way of saying, *No, you wouldn't, my handsome*, whenever Dante boasted about what he would accomplish if he were a politician instead of a photographer.

Antonia was unusually quiet throughout dinner and, though she smiled at Dante's loquacious jokes, she chose to retire early and we left immediately after coffee.

"How did you like the new girlfriend?" I asked her on the way home.

"She's not a *girlfriend*," she said.

"What is she?"

"A tart."

Back home she leashed the dog and rushed out of the house as if she were suffocating. She returned to find me upstairs, sitting on the edge of the bed, lighting one of her Marlboros for her.

"Thank you," she said, as she placed it between her lips and sat at her dressing table to remove her makeup. I rose, walked toward her, and brushed the side of her neck with my lips. But she seemed to shrink away from the unwanted caress. When she took refuge in the bathroom, the click of a closed door rebuffed my aching need to touch her, to lift whatever barrier separated us.

In bed, I waited a long time before she came back. When she felt my hand reaching over to caress her breasts, she moved to the far edge of the bed.

"A good-night to you, too," I said, but she had already tucked her face deep into the pillow.

We both mimicked sleep, struggling to sort out a puzzle which had broken down into far too many intricate pieces.

THIRTEEN

June 9, 2005

Shortly after we met her, he began to call her Sunshine, which may sound a bit tacky in English but is rather romantic in Italian. *Sole.* Like the song. *O sole mio.* She called him Danilo, because she thought he shouldn't be burdened with the monumental responsibility of sharing the name of the Italian master.

"You mean Allighieri?" Dante asked.

"Who else?" Antonia retorted. "There's one Dante. One *Divina Comedia.*"

"That's where you're wrong," Dante argued. "There may be one divine comedy, but there are many, many interpretations."

"Meaning?"

"Never mind," I said, making a valiant effort to inject myself into the dialogue. "Dante enjoys being obscure."

"Still," Antonia insisted. "It's a mistake to compete with the master."

"Compete for what?" Dante asked.

"For the origins of your name," Antonia told him. "There was one Dante then. There is one Danilo now. And that's you."

Not that Danilo had any wish to compete with any master, medieval or contemporary, about anything as holy as his worship of a woman's beauty.

Now, Antonia and I drove to *L'Incontro*, the elegant Italian restaurant on Pimlico Road that Dante, disdainful of my offer of poppadoms and Bombay duck, had suggested. "I hear they have *Stufato di Calamari*," Antonia said.

"Not my favourite, I'm afraid."

"All those wiggly arms put you off?"

"Exactly."

"Then I'll share the stew with Danilo."

"And I'll get stuck with the *gnocchi*."

Antonia laughed and, unexpectedly, leaned over and kissed my cheek. She was wearing the same tight sweater and revealing little skirt which had prompted Dante, a week earlier, to exclaim, "Men kill for a body like that, right, Trev?"

We were stopped at a light, so I took my hand off the steering wheel and stroked her cheek. Though her face remained stony, her fingers pleated and unpleated her silk skirt.

"So?" I asked, as the flow of traffic put us behind a red-currant Bentley with an uncommon Monte Carlo license plate MC 707. An exhibitionist, perhaps? Or merely an Arabian prince, an arms dealer, a pop star.

"So what?" Antonia demanded.

"What do you think about the rumours?"

"What rumours?"

"About you and Danilo."

She took a breath but did not speak.

"I'm sure you've heard," I said. "Everyone else has."

"Who's everyone?"

"Friends, clients, acquaintances. Phoebe Gray, our neighbour down the road. Keith Smythe –"

"He's a gambler."

"And a gossip. Every bit as poisonous as Josephine."

"Oh, that lesbian. She glistens like an apple whenever she sees me."

"So you and Danilo are being tossed back and forth between a gossip and a lesbian."

She seemed to be considering whether to abandon pretence or remain guarded. "Foolish question, Trevor," she said at last. "If the rumours are true and I deny them, you won't believe me. If they're false, it doesn't matter what I say."

"Is that something he taught you? To muddle the issue?"

"Damn it!" she exploded. "You're trying to provoke me, aren't you? You're so damn jealous you don't even understand what it means to be accused of infidelity… to have a finger pointed at you by some idiots who fabricate rumours."

At this I lost my temper and shouted, "Are you saying the rumours aren't true?"

"Watch out!" she screamed, as the Jaguar veered off the road, climbed onto the curb and almost collided with a van.

"Sorry," I said, regaining control of the car. "I don't know what –"

"Go to hell, Trevor," she said.

"Long way away," I said. "But there's one place that isn't."

I had swerved the car, made a U-turn on Regent Street and was speeding back toward Chester Crescent.

"Where are we going?" Antonia asked, her hands braced on the dashboard.

"Home."

"Why?"

"To put those rumours to rest."

"What about *L'Incontro*?"

"What about it?"

"Danilo will be anxious."

"Of course. He's not stupid."

We never made it to the bedroom upstairs. I ripped off her skirt and underpants and thrust her onto her back on the library carpet. She was dry, unready, but I plunged into her furiously, so deep that she cried out and tried to drive me away, both palms jammed against my jaw, and her hips trying and failing to slip away from each thrust.

"Damn you," she groaned. "You're… always… hurting me."

"What about *him*? Are you blissfully happy when he hurts you?"

The commotion had attracted the dog, who pounced on my back, growling and pawing. His trespassing so enraged me I reached behind me, grabbed him by the neck and flung him across the room, where he landed on the hearth, yelping.

"Get off me," Antonia sobbed, her tears running down her cheeks.

But I plunged deeper still, as my thrusting inside her carried me to the edge of a drunken climax.

"Come," I groaned, crushing her lips with mine.

But her face jerked away, the only part of her impaled body she could control.

"Use me," she said. "And get out."

Afterwards I had nothing to say. I left her lying curled up on her side on the library floor and drove to *L'Incontro* where I found Dante comfortably seated on a banquette. The wall behind him was just as I remembered it: handsomely decorated with black and white pictures of famous encounters. Dante had finished dinner and was waiting for his *tiramisu* and espresso.

"Traffic?" he asked.

"No," I said, as I sat across from him. "Life gets chaotic when you're married to a temperamental Italian woman."

But he refused to take the bait.

"They have *gnocchi*," he said.

"I'm starving," I told him. "I think I'll have the filet mignon in a red wine sauce."

"Excellent," the waiter approved and scribbled on his pad. "Will there be a third party?"

"Maybe," I said. "My wife is rather unpredictable." And, turning to Dante, I grinned, "Don't you agree?"

Dante declined to agree or disagree. He offered me the wine menu and sipped his coffee. Though he kept looking over my shoulder at the entrance, he never asked why Antonia wasn't with me.

FOURTEEN

June 8, 2005

Two signs, not far from one another. FUNERAL HOME, with its mysterious elements. Embalming oil, plastic flowers. And BAR, squarish and enticing, the three neon letters glowing purple against the white façade. It was nine forty-five at night when I stumbled in.

"I need a drink," I said, in a voice that wheezed from somewhere deep in my larynx. But the bartender ignored me and kept rinsing glasses, tilting them to catch the light above the counter.

"I need to get fucking drunk," I said to him, as I clambered onto a stool, still clutching the parcel, coarse brown paper against my sweaty palm.

He heard me say it, but for all the response I got, I could have been talking to a granite wall.

"Don't give up on him, mate," an old man grumbled from the next stool. "He'll take your order in his own good time."

He had bushy white eyebrows that sprouted from under a brown beret and fine fingers that kept stirring a frothy drink of a dubious beige hue.

"Looks like rat poison," I said, pointing at the concoction.

"Brandy Alexander," he said. "Mild as milkshake. Want one?"

I shook my head and laid the parcel down on the counter top. "I need to get drunk fast."

"That's quite obvious."

"My wife is in bed with another man," I told him.

"How do you know?" he asked, matter-of-factly.

"I found them."

"What did they say?"

"Nothing. They were fast asleep."

The old geezer nodded sympathetically and shouted to the bartender. "Hey, Rambo. Give this man a drink." Turning to me he asked, "What will it be, mate?"

"Whisky," I said.

He watched as I gulped it down; then his voice grew indignant. "Whores," he said. "They're all the same."

"I haven't told you the bottom line," I said.

"Who cares? A whore is a whore."

"This other man is my best friend."

"Was."

"Yeah. Was."

"You know what she'll say when you ask her, Why him? She'll say, If it hadn't been him, it would have been some other bloke."

"Maybe," I said.

"Whores," he repeated, enraged. "I'd napalm the whole bloody lot."

It was after midnight when I left the bar and roamed the streets like a tramp, too drunk to know where I was going, but not drunk enough to forget what I had seen. At last, I checked into a modest, out-of-the-way hotel in Piccadilly. I was still carrying the parcel which contained the Heathcote painting that was indirectly responsible for my misfortune.

Drunk as I was, I locked the room and looked for a place both secure and suitable. It meant turning from chair to wardrobe to floor, thinking not of the Heathcote itself but of the vicissitudes of life.

"We all mutate," I said to the figure within the brown parcel. "But you wouldn't like it if the hotel caught fire, would you? You'd turn into a handful of ashes, wouldn't you?"

At last, having leaned the parcel against the wall, where nothing would rattle it except an earthquake, I dropped fully clothed onto the lumpy mattress and, mercifully, fell asleep.

FIFTEEN

June 8, 2005

"What an interesting painting," Antonia said. "Is it a Matisse?"

"No," I told her. "Peregrine Heathcote. A young London artist Josephine discovered."

We had finished breakfast, and I was standing at our kitchen counter, preparing to wrap the painting in layers of protective covering for transport.

"How did she discover him?" Antonia asked.

"She saw a TV interview, contacted him, and offered him a show."

"What, exactly, is the woman doing?"

"Looking through her binoculars."

"Obviously. But what is she looking *at*?"

"We don't know. But, since the painting is titled IN SEARCH OF A DREAM, we can draw our own conclusions."

"I think she's looking at something that isn't there."

"Possibly. Pass me that ball of string, will you?"

"Why are you wrapping it?"

"I'm taking it to Brighton," I explained. "The Brighton Gallery is coughing up £20,000. Hell of a lot to pay for a dream, isn't it?"

After what seemed too long a pause, Antonia asked, "When?"

"When what?"

"When are you taking it to Brighton?"

"This afternoon. I thought I mentioned it to you. Sorry if I didn't."

Again that puzzling silence, until Antonia turned from me and lit a Marlboro.

"I'll miss you," she said, in a voice full of smoke.

I looked over at her, surprised by her tone, and realized that I had sensed a certain strangeness I had not noticed before – a flutter in her voice, a reluctance to look at me as we spoke, a nervous tapping of her fingers on the window sill.

"You want to come with me?" I asked.

"No. It's business for you. I would only be in the way."

"You'll be alright on your own, won't you?"

"Of course. And I have Cappuccino to keep me company."

Halfway to Brighton, the driver answered the car telephone. "It's for you, sir," he said.

"Hullo, Trevor? Rufus here. Brighton Gallery. Infuriating, I'm afraid, but I'm on my way to Paris."

"To Paris?"

"Many regrets, old boy, but… well, the *Louvre* doesn't give any options. Try to win French hearts and minds. Bloody impossible. How is next Thursday?"

"Fine, I suppose."

"Sorry for the inconvenience."

"Change of plans," I said to the driver. "We're going back to London."

"Very well, sir."

I looked at my watch and saw that it was just after six. I rang Antonia at home but got no answer. For a woman who didn't mind walking the dog dozens of times, she certainly exceeded her own dog-walking duties. I waited a short time and tried again. No answer.

Not wanting to come into an empty house (and the leftover salmon in the fridge), I instructed the driver to take me to Simpson's for dinner, wait and bring me back to Chester Crescent.

It was almost nine o'clock when I got home. Cappuccino's growl greeted me from the library, which was rather odd since he was accustomed to sleeping on a cushion in our bedroom.

"You silly dog," I said, pleased by his apparent exile. "You're a nuisance to Antonia, not just to me." I laid down the painting on the desk to open the window and get some fresh air into a roomful of smoke.

I was not surprised to find the porcelain ashtray choked with cigarette butts. If anything was strange at all, it was not the beastly cigarette ash spilling over the desk, but the fact that some butts had lipstick marks on them, others didn't.

I emptied the ashtray, tucked the painting under my arm and tiptoed up the stairs, not wanting to wake Antonia. But going up I felt like a child climbing a tree with fragile branches – that something might snap and break. The bedroom was dark but for the fluttery light of a perfumed candle. Jasmine. Her favourite. A tiny flame in a darkness that allowed me in only to shatter my life.

For she was not alone.

They were both naked, the clothes they must have wrenched off each other strewn all over the floor. Dante's red socks entangled with Antonia's black lace bra.

His handsome dark head was resting on her breasts, as if she had succumbed to him lying on her back, yet holding him imprisoned in her arms, so he would not lift away from her. He stirred a little at the sound of my footsteps, then seemed to sink more heavily against her, quickly brushing her nipples with his lips. I backed away.

Fleeing down the stairs, I swallowed what tasted like bile but kept going down, fast enough to feel I was flying blind.

Cappuccino was growling and whimpering and scratching at the front door, wanting to go out. I held him back with the hand that was not carrying the painting. Then, I opened the door and rushed out into the night.

SIXTEEN

June 6, 2005

When I arrived at the gallery, Josephine Tompkinson was arguing with whoever was at the other end of the line. Then she slammed the phone down. "That art vulture, Rufus whatever, wants the Heathcote, but he wants it delivered to his doorstep."

"That's alright, isn't it?"

"If *you* don't mind getting saddled with a trip to Brighton. I'm unable to oblige."

"I'll see what I can do," I told her and dashed away from her angry stare.

Surprisingly, she followed me into the room in the back that served as my office and said, "This is not going to be easy. But it's my duty to try."

"Try what?"

"To rescue you from your pathetic situation."

"Me?"

"Yes, cherub. You."

We were interrupted by the arrival of two elegant Japanese men in impeccable navy blazers. They were looking at the catalogue and pointing at Heathcote's PRIVATE ENCLOSURE which depicted a beautiful woman under a parasol, perched on the bonnet of an antique Rolls.

"Well, I'll be damned," Josephine whispered. "That's Akiro Makasawi, the notorious art dealer from Tokyo."

"Notorious?"

"For always getting what he wants. There are plenty of Westerners who wish they could master his technique. But I'm every bit as clever. And so are you. Bit unscrupulous, both of us."

"That's why we're called dealers."

She dashed out to meet them and they both bowed to her.

"This work is a breakthrough in Heathcote's career," the older one, obviously Makasawi, said.

"Indeed," his partner agreed. "Hedonism and nostalgia. An interesting theme."

"We had a tip-off in Tokyo," Makasawi said. "We go to great lengths to follow a Heathcote."

"How much?" Makasawi asked.

"I'm afraid it's been sold," Josephine said, spinning gracefully as I came out of my office and greeted them with a reverential bow.

"That one is available," I said, pointing at another Heathcote, rather similar in approach.

The two Japanese exchanged comments in their own language, then Makasawi said, "You sell this one to the other client. PRIVATE ENCLOSURE to us."

"That may be a bit difficult," Josephine said.

"But not impossible," the visitor argued, far from discouraged.

"Exactly," I said. "That's my job in the gallery. To negotiate what's negotiable and what isn't."

Josephine laughed. "Pinched the formula from my own father."

Again the private exchange, followed by a question too courteous to seem indiscreet. "How much did your lucky client pay for this magnificent Heathcote?"

"20,000."

"Pounds?"

"Pounds."

"We're prepared to pay forty," Makasawi concluded, and took out his chequebook and fountain pen.

The transaction took a few minutes, after which Josephine allowed herself a hint of scrupulous concern. "Rufus won't mind the swap, will he?"

"Not a bit," I said. "He will be happy to get any Heathcote at such a competitive price."

But Josephine seemed preoccupied with our unfinished dialogue. "Where were we?" she asked, as she followed me back into my office.

"*Pathetic situation*," I prompted her.

"Ah, yes," Josephine said and went on quickly, as if afraid she might lose her nerve. "It concerns your lothario friend and that wilting violet he's having an affair with."

"Which wilting violet?"

"The one you're married to."

The disclosure caused no discomfort in me for the simple reason that I didn't believe it. By no stretch of my imagination could I accept that the two human beings I trusted most in the world were cheating, lying, hiding, and making a fool out of me. In fact, my feeling for Josephine, as she stood bristling in her corner, was one of contempt touched with slight repulsion.

"You don't believe me, do you?" she said.

"Well…"

"Nice lad. Innocent, trusting."

She seemed to expect that her remark would end the discussion, but I fired the obvious question. "What's the proof?"

"Nothing tangible."

"So," I insisted. "Who's calling them culprits? Someone who has no tapes, no photographs, no proof, only a disgruntled suspicion and the bad manners to express it."

"Dear God," Josephine snorted. "I'm really too busy for all this nonsense. And you're too daft to recognize a frontal assault on your honour."

And she stomped out of the gallery.

SEVENTEEN

May 12, 2005

Sunday morning: a corner of paradise. The sky, radiant blue beyond the bedroom window, a hint of sunshine flickering on the wall, Antonia in her négligé, her face inches from mine on the king-size pillow, her opulent flesh hidden under the sheets except for her bare breasts freshly exposed as she turned over.

"Antonia. Are you asleep?"

"I was. What time is it?"

"Half-past nine. Want to get up?"

"Can't think of a good reason."

"Breakfast."

"Who's making it?"

"My turn."

"Good. Then I can take a bath."

I went down the two floors to the kitchen and

marvelled at their elegance. I had admired this Regent's Park townhouse for a long time and had jumped at the opportunity to buy it, hiring an architect to gut and re-design it. The result pleased me, as it combined opulence and simplicity, though the emerald greens and sapphire blues might seem too fiery, too brash, to a more sedate individual.

"Eggs and bacon, or oatmeal with fruit," I shouted, so Antonia would hear me in the bath, steaming with her mineral salts.

But she surprised me by coming down the stairs, already dressed in jeans and a pullover.

"What is it?" I asked.

"I heard something scratching at the door," she said, and stepped out to the garden in front.

I broke the eggs into a bowl, scrambled them and dropped them into the sizzling butter. A cool breeze shook the tulips, trapped in their ceramic vase on the kitchen table. Petals dropped as the front door slammed shut and Antonia came into the kitchen, holding a scruffy bundle in her arms.

"Someone must have left the poor thing here," she said.

"No collar?"

"No."

"It's probably lost. We'll call the animal shelter and try to find its owner."

"I don't think so, Trevor. Whoever left him doesn't want him. Perhaps because he's a cripple."

The dog was squealing and squirming and trying to jump out of Antonia's arms.

"Something's wrong with his front left paw," she said, trying to examine it as the dog gave a loud growl. "Looks shorter than the others."

"Christ, you're right," I said, as I looked at the stump and realized with a touch of guilty annoyance that I regarded the dog as an intruder, a claim on Antonia that disrupted our perfect solitary twosome.

"It's filthy," I said. "Didn't leave the fleas behind when it came in, did it?"

"I'll clean him," Antonia said. "All that's needed is a little kindness *e niente di piú.*"

Embarrassed, I feigned a spark of enthusiasm. "Certainly. Whatever you… Shit! The eggs are burning!"

While I tried to scrape the burnt eggs from the bottom of the pan, Antonia fed and scrubbed the dog so there was not a fleck of dirt on him. She found a newspaper bin, which she emptied and lined with a towel. When she was finished, the little bugger looked surprisingly pert despite his snivelly snout and lame leg and ridiculous stub of a tail.

"We'll name him Tiberius," Antonia declared with a smile of accomplishment, as the dog sniffed his new lair.

But when Dante arrived that evening to join us for supper, he frowned at the new arrival and shook his head.

"Such a pompous name for an ordinary little dog," he said.

"You agree, Trevor?" Antonia asked.

"Does seem a bit deceptive," I said, perversely pleased that Dante shared my displeasure.

"What shall we call him?" she asked, with her most mischievous smile, letting us know that the dog was here to stay, whatever name was bestowed on him.

"*Bristles*," I said.

"*Riccio*," Dante suggested, echoing my thoughts.

"Hedgehog!" Antonia protested. "Awful name for this cute beagle."

"Not a beagle," I said. "A long-haired Jack Russell. They're quite snappy, you know."

Even as I spoke the intruder got up from his bin and limped over to where the three of us sat. I was not yet accustomed to such shrill barking, made worse by his using his sharp claws to punish the chintz on the library sofa.

"He does have a handsome coat," Dante

admitted, as if humouring Antonia. "Tan and white, like a cappuccino with a dash of nutmeg."

"That's it!" Antonia squealed. "Cappuccino! That's his name."

After consuming three bottles of *Brunello di Montalcino* 1999, we agreed that a dog should be identified by his name. And a man by his dog.

"And a woman?" Antonia asked, with a tipsy giggle.

"By her claws," I said.

"No," Dante disagreed. "By her scent, her allure, her –"

"Right," I said. "We get the drift."

EIGHTEEN

May 8, 2005

Whenever I think of Florida – which is not very often – I think of tropical storms, orange groves, tiny salamanders scampering about with fiercely curled tails. And, of course, Palm Beach, that 14-mile long "strip of paradise," which my grudging memory recognizes as our ancestral home, Dante's and mine, our lean adolescent bodies coiled quietly on the Atlantic sand.

"You know, Trev, if my mother marries that Brit, she'll move to England."

That was during summer vacation between freshman and sophomore years at Everglades High. How many times had we faced the possibility of his moving away? Many. But this one seemed more serious than usual.

"He's loaded, huh?" I said.

"Which means you and me will go too."

"*You* will. Not me."

"I won't go without you."

"You may have to, Dante. I can't leave my dad behind."

"He won't care. He'll go on selling insurance and –"

"Getting trashed, I know. But I can't walk out on him. He's already been dumped once."

By my mother. Who went out to buy bread and milk and never came back. Almost four years ago. A postcard had arrived from North Carolina, saying, *Sorry. Tired of dealing with penniless trash.* Nothing more. Ever again. My father didn't complain. He worked hard. Drank heavily. Stared into the infinite. But he wasn't someone you could walk away from. Not if you had an ounce of pity.

Dante dropped the discussion, but tried again a few days later. "If you stay here," he said, "you'll never be rich, because the rich don't get stuck in some shit hole. They leave stuff behind. Move on. Get richer."

Thinking of Palm Beach is a bit of a riddle. Puzzling and, at times, utterly mystifying. In our expectant adolescence, the island's wealth was captivating to us. Dante and I were intrigued by Flagler, Mizner, and the Moorish-Mediterranean mansions that bore these architects' names. We were just as curious about the shops along Worth Avenue and the courtyard streets, Via Mizner, Via Parigi, among others. And we were fascinated by the famed heiress, Marjorie Merriweather Post, and her multimillion dollar mansion *Mar-a-Lago*, with its own tunnel to the beach.

Above all, there was one thing in Florida that Dante was passionate about: its flora, dwarfed in my own memory as nothing more than clumps of bougainvillea and the odd hibiscus bush. No wonder he got A's in Botany, ultimately surpassing our teacher's ability to draw and identify oleander, jasmine, juniper, yellow elder, honeysuckle, schef-flera, *exceptis excipiendis*.

Over the course of several summers, Dante and I managed to "pinch" a few oranges off the neighbour's tree – if it survived the frost. It always did, which meant we would get the full benefit of its crop – or as much as we could steal.

Though we scented danger in the furious growling beyond the fence, our excursions yielded surprisingly delicious oranges until the day the neighbour, Mrs. Sheridan, unleashed her dog on us. She was a shrivelled old lady with skin like that of an iguana, permanently annoyed with being pestered, and forever mumbling, "Holy Moses, I hate those little pricks."

The dog – half mastiff, half God-knows-what – seized my ankle as I was climbing down from the tree and sank his teeth into my flesh. My screams prompted Mrs. Sheridan to appear in her back yard and show some mercy, "Let go, Kimball. Let go, boy."

But the dog, in his blind fury, bit harder before he released me. As I painfully pulled my ankle away, it revealed four red tooth marks and a bloodied saliva-spattered foot. The wooden fence we climbed to get away was shaky and full of splinters, and our retreat mimicked that of two scurrying rodents punished further by Mrs. Sheridan's angry snarl, "Where's the mother? Don't they have a fucking mother?"

* * *

"Hey, wake up," Dante said, as he joined me in our usual booth at the exotic dance club in Piccadilly where we occasionally indulged (without Antonia) in a floor show that featured striptease.

"You'll never guess what I was thinking about," I said.

"Florida," he retorted. "You always have that look on your face when you think about Florida."

"What look?"

"Oh, I don't know. Searching for memories?"

"You're right. I was thinking about that bloody witch, Mrs. Sheridan, when she sent her dog after me. You remember that?"

"Of course. We must have been about ten."

The lights went down and someone shouted, "Hush!" as a gorgeous woman in a leopard skin suit sauntered onto the stage, clung to a pole and arched her body like an acrobat.

"Didn't change our ways though, did it?" I said.

"Hell, no," Dante laughed, as we were hushed again by several angry patrons.

NINETEEN

April 27, 2005

We couldn't go directly to *Annabel's* for dinner, as we would have arrived wet and bedraggled from being caught in the rain. But there was an advantage to stopping at home first. Antonia made herself stunningly beautiful, pausing in front of the mirror to inspect her *décolleté*, the string of pearls around her neck, the smudge of brown shadow on her eyelids.

Dante was already waiting for us at his usual table near the FIRE EXIT. "Bit uncalled for, isn't it?" I had remarked at an earlier date. "Doubt there're any pyromaniacs at *Annabel's*."

"Best to be prepared," he had replied with enough irritation in his voice to suggest that we drop the subject.

Though he was eager to taunt us with the promised news, he did acknowledge Antonia's beauty with a wolf whistle that belonged far more in a dark corner of the Via Veneto in Rome, than in the sacrosanct interior of this private club in London. Despite its enormous popularity, I regarded *Annabel's* as just another crowded hot spot for the rich and famous. Not that I minded being there – it amused Antonia and gave Dante a chance to lavish a fortune on our meal.

After the waiter had poured from the *Dom Perignon* cooling in the ice bucket, Dante took his usual oblique path to the announcement.

"Well," he said. "What do you do when you inherit a valuable art collection?"

You needn't be a genius to read Dante's mind, but I pretended not to know what might be wrapped in the mysterious package he was holding in front of him, as if he had just seized a coffer with the Crown Jewels.

"No idea." I said.

"What about you?" he asked Antonia.

"I think it's a gift for us," she said.

"Smart woman," Dante said, beaming. "That's exactly what it is. A wedding gift for my best friends."

Interesting. Antonia and I had been married almost three and a half months, but he was now bringing presents to the "newlyweds."

"Show us what's in the parcel," I said.

But Antonia had taken out a Marlboro and was waiting for a light (from Dante's lighter since I, a non-smoker, did not carry one). She grazed the back of his hand with her fingertips and blew out a cloud of smoke shaped like a sail in the wind.

"What about the parcel?" I asked.

Long minutes went by as Antonia struggled to undo the wrapping. But, when she did, the painting took my breath away.

"Basket of lemons, early Matisse," Dante said. "Doesn't come from my stepfather's collection. This one I bid for –"

"We can't accept it," Antonia declared.

"Why not?" Dante asked.

"It's too valuable," she replied, spilling a bit of ash on the tablecloth. As she flicked it off with a pensive smile, she added, "Give us a candlestick, or a silver frame."

"Nonsense," Dante said. "Tell her, Trev."

"Tell her what?"

"That a small Matisse is a trifle compared to the value of friendship." He paused, then added a possessive pronoun to his remark, "Of *our* friendship."

"True," I said, my voice breaking a little, as I rose

and walked around the table to give him an awkward hug.

Over his shoulder I saw Antonia staring at the painting. She was silent, but the look in her eyes gave away her inner struggle – a range of emotions that must be as troubling as it was pleasurable.

"Remember the lemon tree in my father's garden?" she asked.

We both said, Yes, we did.

TWENTY

April 27, 2005

My hopes for a perfect Wednesday afternoon were dashed when I saw heavy clouds dimming the sun with a veil of grey.

"I didn't bring an umbrella," I said to Antonia, as we approached the Chester Road entrance to Regent's Park.

"You think it might rain?" she asked.

"Looks dark."

"What can rain do? Except get us wet."

"Precisely."

She laughed and we kept on going. Regent's Park, at five this afternoon, was crowded with tourists, photographers, students and nature lovers enthralled by the rhythms of spring. The cherry blossoms were utterly still, as if waiting for the breeze that would flutter them out of their calmness. We made our way to our favourite stream and I leaned closer to her as she fed the swans.

"Antonia," I said, with that strange fear that seized me from time to time, "You still love me?"

"Of course."

She didn't look at me but followed the trajectory of the bigger swan, the male, as he beat his mate to a piece of stale bread."

"*Cattivo*," she yelled.

"That *was* rather nasty," I agreed.

But I was far more interested in us than in the behaviour of swans.

"And you have no regrets?" I said.

"I didn't say that. I do have some."

"Such as?"

"Leaving my father, obviously."

"Apart from him?"

"The brown soil, the wild nature, the Amalfi cliffs –"

"But you agree there are similarities between our two countries."

"Such as?"

"The trees, the flowers, the blue of the sky, the sprawling beauty of the parks –"

"No crickets."

"A few."

"But we have millions."

Again, I felt that fierce urge to tear her away from her Italian roots, her memories, and transplant her, now and forever, to the not so flamboyant but equally fertile British soil. For, rootless, she was more likely to drift toward me, to become my muse, my fetish, my possession. Belonging was what she knew best. If not to her father, then to her husband.

Odd as this might seem, it came down to a very simple premise. The love object would not exist without the lover who created it.

As we watched the swans drift away, I suppressed my inner agitation and focused on seizing any morsels of insight she might be willing to reveal.

"What do you miss most about Anacapri?" I asked.

"Songs."

"I'll take voice lessons. Guitar lessons. I'll sing under your balcony."

"*Vermicelli* with sautéed clams."

"Italian shops import it and restaurants make their own."

"I also miss that moment at midnight, when you look up and see a *luna caprese*."

Hearing this, I dropped down to my knees and belted out in my loudest baritone the only words I could remember of the song she loved: *Luna, luna caprese.*

She burst out laughing and I stared at her, as if I had been asleep all my life and only now had awakened. But the idyllic mood was not meant to last, for no sooner had the wind blown a cool gust through the weeping willows, than a thunderclap, with its jagged zigzag of lightning, rolled away from the clouds.

"*Che bruto tempo!*" Antonia exclaimed, as the rain began to fall, stripping the flowering trees of their blossoms and forcing us to run for shelter under a nearby gazebo.

"Let's go to the movies," I suggested, having observed her fascination with whatever romantic Italian movie, no matter how ancient, was captured in celluloid. "There's an old Fellini playing in Camden."

"Since when do you like the movies?" she asked.

"Since we were caught in the rain."

Again she laughed: a throaty flirtatious sound that mirrored happiness and was, therefore, easily mistaken for it. Her mirth was interrupted by the ringing of my mobile. Dante, sounding mysterious, asked if we would join him at *Annabel's*. Wouldn't say why. Would only say that the table would be set for celebration. With a capital C.

"We've been ordered to join Dante at *Annabel's*," I said to Antonia. "You don't mind, do you?"

"I certainly do," she said. "Does he think he owns us?"

As always, I was vaguely concerned that, unknown to herself, her petulant distaste might mask the fascination Dante exerted over women. Somewhere in Freudian pharmacopoeia, wasn't the love potion brewed in a desire to overcome rejection?

"Dante is celebrating," I explained, making room for other rain-soaked couples hurrying into the gazebo.

"What?" Antonia sneered. "Burning up his step-father's money?"

I was unused to such a harsh response and would have preferred to humour her, even if it meant sitting through a foreign flick in some small crowded cinema. But, somehow, I felt I owed it to Dante to persuade her.

"You know what he's like," I said, attempting to sound conciliatory. "Bit manipulative. Even bossy. But he's genuinely fond of us."

"I think we should find him his own girl."

"He doesn't want a girl. He wants many. He needs to be able to walk away when it's over."

"So like an Italian."

"Well, you know what they say. If it walks like a duck and talks like a duck –"

"It will roast like a duck," Antonia said angrily, as we dashed in the rain to hail a passing taxi.

TWENTY-ONE

April 3, 2005

Pope John Paul II was dying in his private quarters at the Vatican, and thousands of pilgrims had flocked to St. Peter's Square to watch the light in his window and pray for his soul.

Antonia, dressed in a long-sleeved sombre black gown and wearing a black lace mantilla, was about to leave our house for the airport and the short flight to Rome when her father phoned to discourage her. Foolishness, he argued, utter foolishness to disrupt your household, only to cast another shadow among thousands in a city that, concerned with security, had erected road blocks and banned new arrivals.

"You won't be able to get through," he said, and went on to explain that Rome was already mourning the Pope's impending departure which, paradoxically, signalled the end of a great man's exile from God.

"Your prayers will reach him from wherever you are," Piero Giordano said to his daughter, with the mystical assurance granted to him by his faith.

Antonia did not challenge his authority. She took off her mantilla and dropped her overnight bag on the library floor and sat in front of the TV, stupefied, wiping her eyes and watching the BBC broadcast of chamber music and hymns.

Though an admirer of the Pope – who was no doubt a great evangelist and defender of the faith – I was not given to succumb to the demands of such remote grief. You needn't be an atheist to reject the religious imperatives of any church, mosque or temple. You need to think of yourself as nothing more than a member of the human race, that mysterious entity on whom life is bestowed and taken away in the same arbitrary manner as that of an insect.

"Hey," Dante said, as he arrived unexpectedly, armed with his ever-present Nikon D80. "I just took some great pictures of the crowds gathering outside Westminster Cathedral."

"Because of the Pope?" I asked.

"Yeah. There's a candlelight vigil for the faithful and a –"

"I want to go." This from Antonia, who had quietly left the library and appeared at the entrance hallway, where Dante was taking off his jacket, ready to relax.

The thought crossed my mind that I should make an effort to comply, but I had no desire to participate in a peaceful eruption of religious grief. "Tompkinson wants me at the gallery," I said.

"Not tonight!" Antonia protested. "How could he?"

"Inventory before taxation," I said lamely, and turned to Dante. "You're both Catholic. Why don't you take her?"

I had expected him to graciously consent to this proposal, but he surprised me by saying, "I'm afraid I can't. I have to develop this film and drop it off –"

"Please," I said. "You can do that later. This is important to Antonia."

Dante nodded, though he seemed embarrassed by my refusal and reluctant to be a pawn in the compromise. But Antonia had already put on her mantilla and was walking to the door with the angry and distraught look of someone who was turning emotional bolts in her brain.

"Off we go, then," Dante said, in the most casual voice he could muster.

If I watched them walk away from the library window, it was simply because I was already lost without them. To my relief, Tompkinson phoned to postpone the inventory. "Everyone is off to Westminster," he said.

I planted myself in front of the televised broadcast of all the candlelight vigils being held throughout the world. Faith was there, so adamant you almost expected to see the pontiff's soul float away from his body and upward into heaven. Which made me wonder if Dante and Antonia had reached their destination. Were they praying? Lighting candles? Holding on to each other so they wouldn't be separated by the multitudes?

I should have gone with them. On this strange night, the house was cold and I felt terribly alone, almost forsaken, at a time when everyone else was sharing that mercurial chemistry they recognized as faith.

And yet, my own had always let me down. Ever since childhood, if not earlier. Perhaps I had grown up too quickly and missed a vital range of emotions. Perhaps those missed emotions had caused me to become a religious misfit – someone who didn't quite succumb to his faith or did so with great reservations.

My faith had taken a series of intricate turns

and, somewhere along the way, the good Lord and I had parted company. Left on my own, I reached the conclusion that an irreverent soul could fly toward the maelstrom of eternity as swiftly as a reverent one, and that whoever had said that faith moved mountains had never been in the Himalayas.

Half-past-eight already. The evening was running away from me. The TV images showed the crowds had grown to large proportions. I could no longer bear to sit still and wait.

I rushed out into the night in search of Dante and Antonia and joined an almost surreal scene outside Westminster Cathedral – strangers embracing, chanting, lighting their candles from those that were already burning and fluttering, crisscrossing each other like fireflies in the darkness.

But the same resolve which had prompted me to look for them also drove me to distraction. How likely was it that I would stumble upon them? Most unlikely, if not impossible.

* * *

It was almost ten when I got back. The house had become darker and emptier during my absence, and my desire for companionship had turned into an ache. Upstairs I changed into my pyjamas and became a philosophical husband again. I had sent them out on a spiritual journey, hadn't I? I hadn't set a curfew for their return. None was needed under such unusual circumstances. My problem, wasn't it, if I was unable to express my religious inadequacies.

But the two of them might not be able to understand. Might find evidence of a pathetically hollow body impervious to the allure of spiritual magic. And, furthermore, my indifference might provide another link between them – remind them they were already joined by their shared Italian heritage and religious faith.

When I woke up at midnight, there was a small flicker of light casting a few stray shadows on the wall that displayed an image of the Virgin Mary and her infant Son. Antonia, kneeling before the votive candle, was clutching her rosary, or so my eyes, confused by the dimness, seemed to perceive.

"Antonia," I called, but when she failed to answer, I rolled out of bed and got down on my knees next to her.

Only then did I realize that, rather than praying,

she was weeping silently into the palms of her hands.

"Please don't be sad," I whispered into her ear.

"Can't help it. I feel so –"

"He was a great Pope. I think he is where he wants to be."

Though she acknowledged my sentiment with a nod, the words seemed to whip up a strange anguish, a sort of painful brimming, as that of left-over tears ready to spill down her cheeks.

TWENTY-TWO

February 10, 2005

I had been going to Honey Dew for almost two years. I liked to think our connection wasn't purely monetary, that there was some sort of feeling between us, an unspoken complicity that a man wiser than myself might not have taken for granted.

"You're late, Trevor," she said, as I rushed into the rented flat in Hampstead.

"Sorry," I said.

Her almond-shaped eyes made bold contact with mine before she leaned over to unbuckle her high-heeled red sandals. She flaunted her slim buttocks – labouring at her profession had not robbed them of their virginal tightness.

I remembered the lust with which I had feasted on her flesh during one of our early encounters on a cold December afternoon, a dusting of snow on the ground and a crescendo of Christmas carols across the street: a sobering intrusion on sexual intoxication. Today there was no snow, no celebratory jingles, no stirrings of lust. Only a need to find an ending that would appease my conscience.

"Wait!" I said, as she reached down to undo her garter belt.

She looked up, puzzled, and frowned at her watch. "Haven't got time, Trevor," she said. "New client from Australia, wants me at Hotel *Athenian* and traffic is a damn good mess."

"You can be a bit late, can't you?"

"No. He wants to get laid before *Phantom of the Opera*. Curtain at eight."

"Please," I begged her. "This is the last time I'm going to see you."

She chuckled with her usual amused complacence. "I've heard that before."

"This time it's different."

It must have been the voice. I had spoken in one of those voices that pleaded for understanding.

"What's wrong, Trevor?" she asked, giving me a worried sideways glance. "You turning prissy? No more Honey Dew? You want faggot with a big willie now?"

"No," I told her. "I'm in love with a woman. I can't get her out of my head."

136

"Is she beautiful?"

"Yes."

"Like me?"

"Different. She's Italian."

"Nice country for vineyards. Not for lovers."

"What do you mean?"

"Italian lovers always promising love. Never keeping promise."

"Am I talking to a world authority on this subject?"

"You talking to Chinese girl who grew up dancing on People's Square. You know how many people?"

"A billion."

"So, Shanghai girl smarter than you. I already married, already ditched, already gone from one madam to another." She paused and shrugged with a mixture of regret and stubborn pride before she went on, "But you don't want sermon. You want that thing locked up in your heart. Chinese people have name for it. Elusive happiness. You catch elusive happiness, I fuck Australian client. You happy, he happy. Me rich."

We did not have sex that afternoon. I told her to go straight to her next assignment. She hesitated, and seemed concerned about my lack of satisfaction, or, perhaps, the finality of our farewell, I couldn't quite fathom which.

I reached out and unclipped her red alligator purse. The bills I tucked into it were crisp, neatly folded, and offered with an earnest desire to be generous, perhaps extravagant.

TWENTY-THREE

January 12, 2005

Seen from the crowded pier of the Marina Grande, the island of Capri rises from the azure of the Mediterranean as if the gods had delivered themselves of an exotic extravaganza. Steep, haughty, calcareous, and shaded by pine trees, the majestic rock has weathered broiling sun, pounding rain and fierce wind to remain a vision of breathless beauty.

But amidst this nocturnal sweep of wind, surf, fog horns and the churning of the inky-black water under the approaching hovercraft, I wasn't pondering the origins of Capri. I was distracted by the two people hugging each other next to me on the quay: Piero Giordano and his daughter (my wife of a full, unquestionable six days). *Mine, all mine.* The thick cascade of charcoal hair, the nape of her neck, the elegant shoulders wedged between Piero's coarse bare arms, much more suited to mending nets than embracing a young woman too beautiful to be his or any other mortal's daughter.

"Don't catch a cold in London's wet weather," he said. "If you do, drink a tisane with lemon and honey."

"I will," she promised. "And you? Will you be alright?"

"Yes," he said, giving her another hug. "Did you remember to pack your hairbrush? The one Aunt Flaminia gave you?"

"Yes. Is she going to look after you?"

"Of course."

"They're ready to raise the plank," I told them, as the sailors unlooped the last of the ropes.

"*Ecco*, Antonia," he said. "*Buon viaggio*. And you, Trevor –"

"Yes, sir."

Smiling as he attempted to explain what he wanted of me, he offered a triumphant V with his fingers and said, "Much better to accept what we don't understand."

I chuckled. Did he mean women in general or Antonia in particular?

"Well, Trevor. I'm talking about that *specie di tortura* we call love."

In parting, Antonia turned once more to her father, who had already withdrawn into the shadows, as if unable to bear the image of the boat backing away from the wharf and already pointed towards Naples.

"*Torniamo subito*," she yelled, and I thought that certain words in certain languages have their own eloquence.

"We *will* come back soon," I reassured her and, watching a few wan lights disappear along the coastline, I added, "See those lights? In every port, all over the world, there are boats leaving, and people like us saying good-bye."

"Sad people," Antonia said.

"Don't be sad. I love you so much."

"So you say. But what *is* this love you feel for me?"

"I can't describe it. It's almost spiritual."

"But not so in bed."

I knew exactly what she meant. Those love exertions on our wedding night had been anything but spiritual. And my efforts, on the nights that followed, to kindle a spark that wasn't there must have seemed callous, if not cruel. Had I been insensitive to her virginal disadvantage? Desperate in my need to enter, to penetrate, to quench my lust?

141

"We need to get used to each other," I said.

She looked up with wet cheeks, a sad smile. "It's the name that's so deceiving," she said.

"The name? What name?"

"*Luna di miele.*"

"Translates into honeymoon."

"I know. That's what makes it deceptive. Not sweet at all."

"It will be," I promised, as I took her in my arms and held her tightly in the night, beneath a black-blue sky with a few isolated stars, like crystal splinters pricking a celestial region as impenetrable as my own wife's face.

TWENTY-FOUR

January 7, 2005

I was the only guest standing on the outdoor terrace of the *Scalinata di Napoli*, the Bed and Breakfast Antonia and I had been obliged to settle for in Naples, having missed the last train to Rome. From where I stood, I could make out the outline of Sorrento, the sea, the *aliscafi* going back and forth from Naples to different destinations.

The breakfast – when it finally arrived – was excellent: slices of fresh pineapple, warm bread, homemade marmalade and a thermos of black coffee with hot milk on the side. I devoured it with the hunger that follows a night of carnal excess.

"*Basta così?*" the waiter enquired as if addressing a starvation victim from Ethiopia.

"Yes, I've had enough," I said, and asked him to prepare a tray of croissants and *caffé latte* that I would take upstairs to my wife.

But when I entered the bedroom I found it empty. Antonia's suitcase was on the unmade bed, packed and ready to be locked. I found no other signs that might reveal what was in her mind. Though reluctant to pry, I peered inside her handbag and saw, next to her passport, a note which she obviously intended for me.

Dear Trevor,
I promised to love you till death do us part.
But I cannot keep my promise. I thought I
could, but I can't.

A.

I read it many times. It confirmed my worst fear concerning Antonia: my flimsy hold on her.

I rushed out of the room in search of her, but stopped halfway down the hallway. *Think*, I said to myself. *You won't stop her from leaving by chaining her to a bedpost.* I went back into the room and examined my options. Calmly. During the long minutes that followed, I learned, with the anguish caused by uncertainty, that I could never bear to lose her, never accept being without her.

At that moment I looked out of the window and caught sight of her. She was sitting on a swing in the small garden downstairs, gently rocking back and forth, moving forward into sunlight, then receding into shadow.

When she saw me approaching with the breakfast tray, she looked up and said, "I'm going home."

"Home? Where?"

"Anacapri. My father's house."

"But we just said good-bye to him."

"I don't care."

"What about us? We're married. We're going home to London."

"I don't want to stay with you."

"Is it because –"

"I don't want to be married," she said, confirming what I was beginning to suspect.

I placed the breakfast tray on the scrubbed pine table nearby and crouched on the wild grass next to the swing as it came to a standstill. I raised my hand to touch her arm, but she shrugged away from it.

"Antonia," I said. "What happened last night was insane. I behaved like a beast. You understand? Beast?"

"*Una bestia.*"

"Yes. There is nothing I can say that will explain to you the fury of my passion. But I can promise you this: it will never happen again."

"I don't believe you."

"You must… because it's true."

She got off the swing and walked away from me. I knew exactly what had prompted her to make such a rash decision, and I was sure she knew it, too. As I rushed after her, I bumped into a boy raking the gravel. The rake flew out of his hands, and he backed away, startled.

"Sorry," I said, and meant it.

Sorry about my unscrupulous behaviour. My animalistic appetite. My failure to restrain myself. Sorry about everything.

"Please, Antonia," I said, as I followed her into the room. "Don't shut me out. This may be our last chance to talk this through."

"I have nothing to say."

"But I do. I want us to forget last night ever happened."

"I can't."

"Please try. Maybe we can start all over again. I believe we can overcome barriers –"

"What barriers?"

"Culture, background, religion. Perhaps even language. I'm willing to do my part."

"What about my feelings? Do they mean nothing to you?"

"On the contrary, they mean everything to me.

Let's not go to Rome. Let's stay here so you can be close to your father."

She looked at me and I sensed a certain relief.

"I made a mistake. That mistake is driving you away. Please, Antonia, if you have it in your heart to forgive me –"

But I saw that she had finished packing and was locking her suitcase. A moment of utter despair descended over me as I leaned my forehead against the windowpane and remained transfixed, waiting for the door to open and close.

When it didn't, I turned around and saw that Antonia was standing by the foot of the bed, looking at me across the room.

"Very difficult," she said. "But it's a sin not to forgive. So I'll try. If we both try, maybe it will all turn out for the best."

TWENTY-FIVE

January 6, 2005

It was evening when we arrived at the train station. We rushed up the stairs to the *Binario* 3 in time to see the red lights of the train disappearing in the distance.

"Damn!" I said. "Was that our train?"

"I think so," Antonia said.

We found the station master, who confirmed the Intercity to Rome had departed at 8.45 p.m.

"But I checked the schedule," I argued. "It was not supposed to leave until nine."

He explained with an amused look on his face that train schedules were not set in concrete; rather, they were constantly updated.

We were still wearing our going-away clothes. Antonia had chosen a blue dress with flowing skirt, a tamarind red shawl and a stylish straw hat tipped over her brow. I had favoured jeans and a blazer, but Dante had raised a protesting hand. "Won't get far in those," he said. So I settled for beige corduroys and an elegant Emilio Pucci jacket. There were grains of rice caught in her hat and in the collar of my open shirt where the tie had been.

The taxi driver understood our predicament and knew immediately where to take us: the *Scalinata di Napoli*, a small Bed and Breakfast which obviously attracted stranded travellers.

I was reluctant to spend our first night together in a shabby waterfront rooming house, surrounded by fake Italian Renaissance furniture, crimson satin curtains and Botticelli prints.

"This place is not what I had in mind," I said.

But Antonia looked tired and drawn. She was sitting on a chair, with one of her shoes off, massaging her foot. "We'll be in Rome in the morning," she said.

There was a smell of burnt caramel in the reception room. The fat matron at the desk raised her head as we approached. Neither our unscheduled arrival nor our elegant clothes seemed to surprise her.

"How many nights?" she asked.

"Just one."

An old man limped over to take our luggage, and

we followed him up two flights of narrow wooden stairs. When I handed him a five euro tip, he snatched it with an arthritic claw and stuffed it inside his shoe.

He left quickly and I chose to pay attention to the room before approaching Antonia. Turn the key in the lock. Open the window. Let the fresh air dispel the mustiness. Draw back the hideous red quilt. Inspect the sheets and pillowcases.

In the large mirror in the room I had a glimpse of myself, nervous but committed, like a hawk, and the back of Antonia's head. She was standing by the window, trying to undo the clasp of her pearl necklace with trembling fingers. When I approached to help, she stiffened and drew away.

"Are you afraid?" I asked.

"Yes," she said. "It's my first time."

"Your first time? Ever?"

"Aunt Flaminia told me that if I lost my virginity, I would never find a husband."

"Unlikely in today's world –"

"She said it happened to her."

I stood silent, looking at the hat she had placed on the dresser, the shawl draped over a chair, and felt that she was, indeed, frightened. That perhaps the romantic notion of a *luna di miele* she may have harboured in her imagination was about to be sabotaged by the sexually aroused male who was standing before her, breathing her in.

"We don't have to do anything more. I'm happy just holding you in my arms."

But, as I said this, I was undoing the many buttons on the front of her dress, fumblingly, one by one.

"My aunt Flaminia says they call it *il nostro amore*, but it's only the man's *amore* that matters. For the woman it's always *a piú tardi*."

"Your aunt Flaminia is wrong," I said, sweeping up the dress to pull it off over her head.

"So, *il nostro amore* –"

"Means yours and mine," I said, unzipping my pants and dropping them to the floor.

The corduroys got caught at my ankles, and I stumbled getting them off. "There's no *later* for those in love," I told her. "It's *now* that counts. Both for you and me."

"So I'm fortunate," she said, removing a hairpin, so that her long mane came tumbling down her shoulders. "I have a man who understands me."

But as I stroked her inner thigh with my finger-tips and inhaled the scent of the perfumed underpants I had pulled off her, the chivalrous within me was overcome by an instinct far more brutal. My prick, stiff with lust, could not bear the agonizing wait for ejaculation. I felt almost barbaric as I lifted her up and cradled her buttocks in my palms and sought to enter, still standing by the window. Her cry of pain was shrill against the clatter of a wheelbarrow moving across the cobblestones.

When I carried her to the bed, shivering, she tried to pull the covers over herself, but I thrust them aside and forced my knee between her thighs until they opened wide and I plunged into her, probing, touching, then labouring in earnest, blotting out all sensation except the approaching frenzy, the mingling of our juices, blood, sweat, saliva, semen, and her tears running down her face onto the pillow, her wound too sore to feel even a flutter of pleasure that would challenge Aunt Flaminia's grim surrender to the savagery of man.

In the morning she was touchingly sprawled across the bed. A slender nymph, sound asleep, oblivious to the chaos which had engendered my lust and overruled her reluctance. As I crept out of the room in search of breakfast, the mirror bared a rather unfamiliar face, half-rapist, half-Eros, a face altogether baffled by that *specie di tortura* we call love.

TWENTY-SIX

January 6, 2005

Certain things I remember vividly, while others have been stamped out of my memory like a wheat field trampled by an ox-cart. A figure in white flits across my vision. White veil. White gown. A bouquet of tiny white roses – only they aren't roses – stephanotis, I think, is their name.

Piero Giordano was wearing polished black shoes with long shoelaces. At first I thought he and the figure in white were miles and miles away; then I saw they were standing next to me at the altar. Antonia's face was eclipsed by yards of white tulle which rendered her features blurred and aloof.

I remember slipping a ring onto Antonia's slender finger. I also remember her frustration at finding mine too thick, too damp, so that she was obliged to twirl the ring, and abandon it below the middle knuckle, where it stayed until I pulled it off and transferred it to the little finger. No longer tight, it was now precariously loose.

The bells were tolling at the baroque Church of Santo Stefano, with its quaint tower and eastern looking cupola, under which the small arcades opened out onto the *piazzetta*. As we descended the steep hillside, Antonia would have fallen if Dante hadn't spun around to catch her.

Did I say it was a perfect wedding? Perhaps not, for, as we arrived at the Giordano household in Anacapri for the reception, there was an anguished (though momentary) commotion caused by Aunt Flaminia's fainting spell. And another, much later, when Cousin Luna latched on to the *carissimo* Mario (the popular cousin who was a notorious flirt) while dancing the tarantella, prompting his wife to throw a glass of red wine in his face.

Most of all, I remember the smell of pine trees, the plaintive lament of Neapolitan songs, my own desire (which I had trouble concealing), urgent, almost abrasive, against the crotch of my grey gabardine trousers. A mouthful of ambrosia cake with almond paste icing. A kiss. Another kiss, this one lingering as I guided Antonia toward the tangle of bodies on the dance floor.

"May I?" the *carissimo* Mario, his grin peeled back upon large teeth, snared my wife and held her tightly against his gut.

I was slow to conclude that I could take her back from him, and when I approached (as they bounced past me from the far end of the dance floor), it had already been done. Dante, in an act of fraternal zeal, had plucked Antonia from Mario's arms and transferred her into his own, causing Mario to grin and utter with infinite empathy, "*Siamo animali, caro amico. Siamo animali.*"

So he understood, as well as I did, that we are indeed animals, that we shed our human pretences in favour of the animalistic tendencies that lie dormant within us.

Antonia was still in Dante's arms during the next dance, and the next one, so I walked back to the bar and stood next to a thin bald man who was drinking champagne with an air of having formed opinions about everything.

"*Un bello marito,*" he said, the glitter of his champagne flute catching the revolving lights in the ceiling.

"He's not the husband," I blurted. "I am."

And walked away, surprised to discover the blunt response had been prompted by the long-existing rivalry between Dante and myself. Had it come to an end? Was I the rightful owner of the woman I had married? Or, merely, the taker of a stolen heart.

TWENTY-SEVEN

December 28, 2004

Pale winter sunlight had begun to filter through the bleak clouds as I stood before the elegant mirror of my bedroom at the *Punta Tragara* Hotel in Capri, and stared at myself, critically, with academic curiosity, eager to determine what would please (or displease) those who held the key to my happiness.

The reflection in the mirror showed my thick blondish hair neatly slicked back and parted on the side. My grey eyes quite serious, concerned that everything should be in order. The lips tight, as if too nervous to smile. The shoulders and arms strong, despite the fidgety hands. In short, a man not gorgeous like Dante, but in possession of an easy bearing and virility, which supported my claim that I was the rock and he the shifting sand.

There was only one thing that could have shaken my confidence at that moment, and there it was, eerie and unequivocal: a crack in the upper left corner of the mirror. I didn't know whether the gods were teasing me or warning me, but either way they had trespassed on my happiness. I stared at the cracked mirror, unable to dispel my deeply superstitious fears.

When the Reception rang to announce that Dante had arrived, I was relieved to go downstairs and meet him.

"Hey, don't look so frightened," he said. "You're not meeting *Barbarossa*, you know."

The day had dawned sullen and grey. An ordinary day, like so many others, and yet what was about to take place was far from ordinary.

"Why are you so nervous?" Dante asked, as we walked the whole length of Via Tragara, toward the *piazetta* where we would take a bus to Anacapri, the village where Antonia lived. "Piero is a decent fellow, and Aunt Flaminia a timid soul. Wouldn't say boo to a goose."

"I'm trying to make sense of the way I feel," I told him. "The reason why I'm so in love with Antonia."

"Her looks, obviously."

"Goes beyond that."

"Well, she's young, unspoiled. She's also motherless, as you are."

"That's a common denominator. Not a reason to marry."

We reached the *piazzetta* and turned left and up the street toward the bus stop.

"This could be just another fling," Dante said. "You've had quite a few, you know."

"Not as many as you."

"Maybe not. But that's because you're always searching for a reason to fall in love. I'm quite happy with a good screw." His voice was vigorous, and the face he turned to me in the drizzle looked eager to move on. "Hurry, Trev. We're about to miss the bus."

Sheltered in the tiny bus, I insisted on carrying the argument a step further. "Perhaps there isn't a reason," I said. "It's like asking, Why are the lilies white? Why is the sky blue? I don't know why. Do you?"

"Of course not."

"Besides," I insisted. "You claim that love is for morons."

"No, I don't," he retorted. "I claim love is for those who are vulnerable to it."

It was the eternal argument between us – one that neither of us ever won.

"That's me? I'm vulnerable?"

"At the moment, yes."

The bus stumbled over a running gutter and stopped, allowing a lorry to navigate past us and keep racing down the hill. I had one quick glimpse of the edge of the cliff, the precipice below. It whipped up the unwanted memory of my father, and I felt a mixture of compassion and distaste. Had he felt terror in the seconds that preceded his fall? Or was he truly ready to annihilate himself?

"Stop thinking about your father," Dante said, as the driver rounded a hairpin turn too fast. "This bus is not going off the cliff. It never has."

"How the hell do you know what I'm thinking?" I asked.

"You're transparent," he answered with a chuckle, and rang the bell which signalled the driver to let us off. The tires screeched and squealed as the bus jolted to a stop.

Across the road, a couple hundred yards into the pine trees, stood a modest villa, with a white gate, a bell and the word GIRASOLE scrawled on a plank above the unglazed wooden door. Through the gate I saw Piero approaching with his ravishing daughter, against canyons of green creeping vines which I mistook for a vineyard.

"He grows his own grapes," I said, admiringly.

"Hardly," Dante snorted. "Those are *campanile*, you idiot."

I had a stray vision of Antonia lying on the rocks of *La Fontelina* the day the clock stopped and my life was changed forever. Now just looking at her as she stood next to her father at the open gate gave me a pang of voluptuous heartache.

"Welcome," Piero said, guiding us down a stone path toward the villa, yet stopping briefly before a niche carved in stone and surrounded by votive candles.

The niche had been undisturbed by the wrath of nature and bore the exquisite image of a young woman who could have been Antonia.

"My mother," she told us.

"Beautiful", Dante said.

"She died when I was born."

Standing in the garden, where a long table had been set for eighteen, the guests (cousins and neighbours of the Giordanos) were nibbling on *focaccia* and drinking wine from large goblets. Aunt Flaminia looked up from adorning the platters with bouquets of parsley. Unlike most middle-aged women on this island, who flaunted ample bosoms and sizeable stomachs, she had maintained a rail-thin frame which in the frenzied capitals of the world might have been mistaken for anorexia.

"*Mi dispiace*, Antonia," she said, in a voice as brittle as her bony shoulder blades. "But I still don't know which of the two *signori* you're marrying."

Before she could answer, Dante blurted, "Both," causing enormous laughter among all present.

My face still stinging from Dante's remark, I wandered toward the kitchen and glimpsed a large squid, madly squirming as it was about to be hacked to death for our gastronomic enjoyment. Though not squeamish by nature, I was unable to watch the *pescatore* who was in charge of carrying out the unpalatable task.

"I'm a vegetarian," I lied, when he offered me a morsel of the unfortunate creature.

The luncheon table had been set with care and devotion. Fresh flowers, linen napkins (showing signs of many washings), various sets of cutlery, earthenware dishes, goblets for white and red wine, crystal flutes for champagne.

"Magnificent," I said to Piero, in an effort to flatter him.

Despite the breezy and faintly cool afternoon we lunched alfresco. The meal started with tomatoes and *fiordilatte*, proceeded with a succulent red snapper caught in the Tyrrhenian sea, *calamari fritti*, roast veal brought in from the Campania countryside, and ended (four hours later) with a *torta caprese* and homemade *limoncello.*

I found at once my appetite to be sluggish. The nerves in my stomach, tense by the nearness of Antonia, the physical wealth of her, made it difficult to swallow and almost impossible to sit through the meal.

"Foreigners are shy about food," a large matron said, stroking the ostrich feathers in her hat.

"Not me," her German husband grinned, as he stuffed a piece of *focaccia* into his mouth and reached out for the wine.

At some point I noticed that Antonia was no longer sitting at the other end of the long table. Neither was Dante. When they failed to return ten minutes later, I excused myself and set off to find them. I passed Aunt Flaminia on the kitchen steps, as she carried two flasks of red wine in one hand and a tray of cheese in the other.

"Have you seen Antonia?" I asked.

"*Il giardino*", she said.

"Hold it, don't move." Dante's voice could be heard from the orchard. As I approached, I saw he was talking to Antonia who was leaning against a lemon tree, smiling at the camera.

"Is this one for posterity?" I demanded, in a surly voice.

"Almost done, Trev," Dante said, clicking away.

A moment later he sauntered off the garden and made his way back to the house.

"Look at the sunset," Antonia said.

She was pointing at the Anacapri countryside against the red horizon, the green of the valley sprinkled with lemon groves, the white villas perched along stretches of rich soil and, miles below, a glimpse of the sparkling sea.

And there, during that fleeting moment stolen in her father's orchard, under a peach tree that would be laden with fruit in the spring, Antonia allowed me to kiss her lips, neck, shoulder, then search for her breasts under her thick woollen sweater and hold them in my hand, the nipples stiffening against my fingertips, a bold caress that shook me to the roots of my being but seemed to leave her perplexed by its primitive urgency. So that when Dante was sent to bring us back to the banquet table for the champagne, she sprang away from me and gazed at him for a long time.

"You can kiss me, too," she said, and added with a playful smile, "Everyone kisses the bride-to-be for good luck."

When he didn't, the silence descended upon us like rolling fog. "Go ahead," I told him. "Kiss her."

There was a silky rustling as she moved toward him. I saw Dante's strong hand pull her slightly in his direction. This time he did not hesitate. His lips touched the cheek he had scarcely dared approach before.

From the banquet table in the garden, the guests added their laughter to the loud uncorking of champagne. Piero's voice could be heard explaining that Antonia was not a convent girl. She was quite grown up, despite her youth.

"*Lei sa quello che può fare e non può fare,*" he said.

But did she? Know what she could do? What she couldn't do?

"Stay with me," I told her, taking her away from Dante's hold. "I'm the one you can trust."

TWENTY-EIGHT

September 12, 2004

Uncertain whether I would meet a hospitable father or a tyrant, I stood before the gate of the small villa, GIRASOLE, and rang the bell.

The man who opened it was older than I expected. He had a handsome, sunburnt face, a strong handshake and a warm smile that suggested he understood everything, that words would be superfluous and add little to the obvious reason for my visit.

"Come in," he said brightly. "We were expecting you."

His English surprised me, as it was quite good, despite his accent; but he, if he noticed my admiration, chose to ignore it. He opened the door wide, giving me a full view of a smart room overlooking his bit of land flanked by lemon groves. Sunshine flooded the wooden floor of this large living room furnished with attractive but discoloured sofas and armchairs, perhaps the result of so many unshuttered windows.

"Come in," he said, again, as I hesitated at the threshold.

"Thank you, Mr. Giardino," I mumbled, stumbling over the words, the doorstep, almost dropping the bunch of assorted flowers I had purchased at the shop on Via Tragara.

"Giordano," he corrected me with a hearty laugh. "*Giardino* means garden."

The woman he introduced as his sister, Flaminia, was thin as a dragonfly, with grey hair tied in a bun, a voice that squealed *Piacere* (no doubt the equivalent of *Pleased to meet you*), and told me I would find Antonia in the *giardino*, giving me, in the first moments of my arrival, full exposure to the rhythmic fluctuations of her language.

I did not, however, find Antonia in the garden and was tempted to retreat into the house, when I felt a ping on my shoulder.

A lemon sailed by.

Then another.

At that moment I spotted Antonia in a tree. She had climbed halfway to the top and was almost hidden by the intertwined branches and fluttery leaves. The exquisite face was convulsed with suppressed laughter and the huge eyes, when they opened, were glowing with amusement.

"Come down, Antonia," I shouted, and stood just beneath her feet. "Or would you rather I climbed the tree?"

She delivered herself of a few more lemons before she leaped down and came crashing against my chest, startling us both.

She moved away immediately.

"Enough lemons to make a barrel of *limoncello*. Help me gather them and take them to Aunt Flaminia."

I was exultant to be picking lemons next to my muse. The ones Antonia chose snapped off easily and were tossed into a lacquered wicker basket the colour of honey. But mine, the little devils, clung to their branch, despite much tugging.

"I grew up next to an orange grove," I told her. "But I don't remember the oranges being so difficult to pick."

"Like this," she said, her fingers expertly twisting the plump yellow lemons from their stem.

"Wait," I said, when we had finished. "Before we go in, there is something I want to tell you."

But her eyes had drifted, over my shoulder and her inquisitive gaze prompted me to ask, "Is anything the matter?"

"Your Italian friend," she said. "I thought he was coming, too."

"He couldn't. He's taking photographs of a fashion show in Positano."

"Why?"

"He's a freelance photographer. Difficult work, in my opinion, but it suits him. Dante does as he chooses."

"Are you also a photographer?"

"I'm a partner in an art gallery. I sell other people's art. Quite a lucrative profession, I'm happy to say. And yet, I would gladly give it up if I could get a job driving the bus to Anacapri." I waited for her to laugh; when she didn't, I asked, "What about you? Do you work?"

"Oh, yes. Every morning I take the bus down to Capri and work at the *Ferragamo* boutique on Via Tragara."

"A favourite hunting ground for tourists, I suppose."

"Only the rich."

"Is that important to you? Being rich?"

"Of course. Being poor leads nowhere. I'm not poor, but I don't have as much money as I need to do what I want."

"Which is?"

"Travel. Visit the beautiful cities of the world. Buy clothes. Jewellery. Move to Rome, perhaps. Capri is a bit provincial. There's more to life than picking lemons."

Perhaps you will. Sometimes wanting something is the key to getting it."

She nodded and began to move away toward the house when she caught a glimpse of something lying on the grass.

"What's that?" she asked.

To my dismay I discovered it was the bunch of flowers I had laid on the ground near the lemon tree. They dribbled and drooped as I picked them up and thrust them into her hand.

"That's what I meant to tell you," I said. "I got these for you because they're a breath of spring. Just as you are."

"Thank you," she said.

She held them the way she would a cumbersome parcel, then tilted her head to one side and said, "So your Italian friend –"

"Dante."

"Is that his name?"

"Danilo. But he likes to be called Dante."

"So he gave up coming to see me to take photographs of pretty girls walking around in pretty clothes."

"Are you disappointed?"

"Surprised. I thought he liked me."

"Of course he does. But perhaps I like you more."

There was a lingering silence that made me feel plain as mud. This was one time when Dante's absence did not work in my favour. As a rule, I became attractive when I was not in his shadow.

"You'll see him tomorrow at the *piazzetta*," I told her, as Aunt Flaminia appeared with a request from Antonia's father to join him for an aperitif.

I followed them both into the house. Somewhere behind us, the setting sun had begun to move away from the garden and, shrill in the fading light, the song of cicadas twitched in the shrubbery.

TWENTY-NINE

September 8, 2004

It was six in the afternoon. Dante and I stood motionless as tin soldiers on the west corner of the *piazzetta* with our back to the site where the Greek colonies established the acropolis between the fourth and fifth centuries B. C. Now, a millennium later, the *piazza* Umberto I, once known as the "little theatre of the world," was fondly nicknamed the *piazzetta*. I was not surprised by its popularity, as it accommodated everyone's moods, in addition to featuring elegant boutiques and outdoor cafés shaded by multicoloured umbrellas.

Dante smoked one of his Marlboros and I wrestled with the bulky issue of *The Daily Telegraph* I had purchased at the corner kiosk.

As the bells stopped tolling, Dante said, "There she is."

Of course I had already seen her – tall, dark-haired, stunning, taking a seat at the *Gran Caffé*, ordering an espresso and pulling a book out of her satchel as if the coffee and the reading were inextricably connected.

"Trevor," Dante whispered very quietly. "Did you hear what I said?"

"Yes."

"Are you ready?"

"Not quite."

"I am," he announced, taking a deep puff from his cigarette and exhaling through the nostrils."

"You go then," I said, though neither one of us moved.

"We said we would approach her together."

"Alright."

"Alright what?"

"Let's go."

Deliberately or not, the young woman's eyes met ours as we walked across the *piazzetta* resembling two maladroit students in a sheepish pursuit that came to a stop just as the ash from Dante's cigarette spilled and fell on the edge of the table, inches away from the ashtray.

"*Signorina*," Dante murmured and cleared his throat.

The young woman looked at him, as I did – she

with curiosity, I with the discomfort created by his blunt approach.

"*Me dispiace, signorina, ma il mio amico vorrei –*"

"I speak English," the young woman said in a husky, yet melodious voice. "A cousin of mine from Amalfi gives me lessons."

"Selfishly, I'm sure," Dante said. "So he can be near you."

She smiled but did not respond. The silence became too uncomfortable, too long. Dante decided that we were in need of a bold move.

"Mind if we sit down?" he asked with a disarming smile, crushing his cigarette in the barrel-shaped ashtray with the word *Campari* printed on the outer rim.

"Please."

As we scrambled for the two chairs flanking her, Dante blurted, "My friend and I think that you look like a Roman vestal."

She did. Her face was even more beautiful with the glow of the setting sun on her cheeks.

"What is a vestal?" she asked.

"A goddess," I told her.

"A virgin," Dante corrected me, with his customary need for contradiction.

"Actually it's both," I argued.

But my annoyance gave way to a furtive

pleasure as she burst out laughing and said, "I can see that you argue about everything. Who wins?"

"Whoever has the most illusions," I said, prompting Dante to give a loud whistle.

"He means the most cunning," he clarified and shouted to the passing waiter, "A bottle of *spumanti*. Three glasses."

"Not for me," the young woman said, gathering her book, satchel and sunglasses. "My father is expecting me home for dinner."

"May we take you?" Dante asked, as we both sprang to our feet, trying to second-guess each other's next move.

But the young woman shook her head, rose and dropped some euros on the table. "No, thank you," she said. "I take the bus to Anacapri."

"Hey," Dante yelled, as she walked away. "Will somebody tell us what's the point of meeting a goddess if all she does is disappear?"

She looked over her shoulder without stopping and called back, "I'm here at the *piazzetta* every afternoon at sunset."

"We don't even know your name," I shouted.

"Antonia."

"Well, well," Dante said, as we watched her get lost in the crowd of tourists and workers going home to Anacapri. "Something tells me you will be here tomorrow, at the appointed time."

"What about you?"

"Of course."

Which brought an end to our conversation. For he, too, was having his own thoughts. None that he wished to share. It made me wonder if he was curious about mine. Did they matter? Or, was he merely pondering his own with his most distant smile. I had once read him like an open book. Were we doomed to become strangers to each other?

THIRTY

September 7, 2004

No need to ask each other which of the two arrows we would follow. We both climbed down the concrete path that began at Via Tragara and kept winding more and more steeply down the cliff, through the pine forest, all the way to the sea, offering glimpses of breathtaking beauty – volcanic rock, an intensely blue sky, the emerald green water, seemingly still yet pulsating with an urgency of its own. When we came to the fork on the path, we headed toward *La Fontelina*, which Dante had renamed The Fountain of Forbidden Dreams the day before, when we had come upon the beautiful young woman sunbathing on the rocks.

"Why forbidden?" I asked him, since we had agreed we would approach her.

"Because," he said, "she is forbidden to one of us."

"Obviously."

"So what are we supposed to do?"

"What we've always done. One of us scores, the other doesn't."

Never an ideal solution. But, since any solution was better than none, we had no alternative but to pursue the same woman with our very different technique: he with charismatic precision and a touch of histrionics, and I with a more sedate, less flamboyant approach.

"You know this is different, Trev. Don't you?"

"Why?" I asked.

"Because we both want her."

For a magic moment I thought I spied her coming out of the sea, dripping water; but as the blur loomed closer, it became somebody else. Seeing the expression on Dante's face confirmed my fear. Plain and simple: she wasn't there.

"Where the hell is she?" he muttered under his breath.

"No idea."

We began searching the rocks, the sea, the path which led to the small boats that lured tourists to the grottoes. Finally, showing me his determined profile as he gazed toward *La Fontelina* restaurant, he said, "Let's find out."

We sat at a small table for two and ordered local white wine and *pesce*. Domenico, the waiter, recognized us from the previous day and uncorked a bottle of *Tiberio* with a friendly smile.

Dante complimented the wine and addressed the waiter with brisk impatience, "Say, Domenico. Who is the beautiful young woman who lies on the rocks?"

"Which one?" Domenico asked. "They all lie on the rocks."

"She looks like a goddess," I told him.

"They all look like a goddess," he retorted.

"But this one reads Moravia," Dante insisted. "She's smart *and* beautiful."

"*Prego*," Domenico said. "*Come si può esere l'uno e l'altro*?"

"That's just it," Dante assured him. "It's quite possible to be one as well as the other. And she's both. But we don't know who she is."

"Ahh," Domenico sighed. "*La signorina* Giordano. She lives with her father and her aunt in Anacapri."

"Do you know their address?"

"No. But she's always at the *piazzetta* around six o'clock in the afternoon. I see her there on my way home from work."

Dante smiled like a cherub, tipped like a tourist

and stood to survey the emerald waters beyond the rocks with the arrogance Barbarossa himself must have displayed while standing beside the turrets of his castle.

THIRTY-ONE

September 6, 2004

The fire in the *Tentazione* nightclub on via Camerelle in Naples merited only a footnote in the British newspapers. But it was fully covered by the Italian press, in particular the *Corriere della Sera*, which reported that one of their photographers, Danilo Terranova, had "miraculously escaped" what they described as "a fireball in Naples."

"Greatly exaggerated, don't you think?" Dante asked, as we finished our lunch at the *Virginello*, in Capri.

"Seems that way," I agreed.

The waiter who brought our coffee said, "They think it was arson."

"Based on what?" Dante asked.

"Someone has come forward to say he saw a man pouring petrol on one of the rooftops."

"Damn," I said. "Hope they catch the bastard."

"They will," the waiter assured us, as he took away our empty wine bottle and glasses.

Dante sipped his coffee and pulled a Marlboro out of his pack.

"You shouldn't smoke," I told him. "Your throat must be raw, judging from my own."

"Right," he said, and put it away. "Say, Trev, I haven't thanked you for –"

"Yes, you have," I told him.

"I thanked you for saving my fucking life. But not for sticking around like Florence Nightingale. I bet Josephine is getting ready to whip you when you get back."

"It's alright. I've spoken to her."

A large Italian family came into the restaurant and cheerful laughter and voices filled the room. From my place of vantage near a front window, I could see the glittering water in the distance and what appeared to be miniature boats making the crossing from Naples. The side window offered a glimpse of the cable car ascending along terraced slopes, flowering fields and bunches of grapes ripening in the vineyards.

"Before we go back to London," Dante said, "I'd like to take another look at the Blue Grotto."

"Again?" I asked, wondering why he was so fascinated by the interior of a grotto that was plagued with overcrowded boats and noisy tourists.

"The old Romans were convinced it was a meeting place for witches and monsters," he said, with a bit of the old mischief returning to his smile. "I've got my camera ready to immortalize –"

"A few flying bats. That's all I've ever seen there. When do you want to go?"

"Tomorrow. The next day. Whenever."

The plans I attempted to make were seldom definite. They were affected by Dante's indecision, perhaps resulting from a routine that included visits to the burn clinic in Naples.

Dante's injuries had been classified as second degree burns to his face, chest and arms. A full recovery with little or no scarring was expected. His overnight stay in the hospital had been prompted by smoke inhalation as much as the actual burns.

My own ignorance in such matters had been frightening enough to cause me to postpone my return to London and offer my assistance.

"Assistance for what?" Dante had asked, in a disgruntled manner.

"Anything you need."

"If you want to push a fucking wheelchair, get yourself another invalid."

Nevertheless, I had stayed in Capri, making trips

to the clinic, the specialist, the pharmacy. Dante disliked my diligence, but did not dare keep me away.

Our talk about the fire, sporadic at first, had ceased almost completely, and, with the healing of Dante's burnt skin, came an urgent and persistent desire to halt any memories, to wipe away from our conversation the most frightening details.

So, when Dante suggested we finish our coffee and go swimming, I made my usual effort to be agreeable.

"Sure," I said. "Shall we go to the *Canzone del Mare*?"

It seemed the logical choice to spend the afternoon as the *Canzone del Mare* (with its romantic name Song of the Sea) had a large swimming pool in addition to rock bathing off its own sheltered coastline.

But Dante disagreed.

"No," he said. "Let's explore the southern coast of the island."

So, ignoring my own preference, I walked with Dante all the way to the end of Via Tragara and down the winding path through the pine forest.

But, before we could reach the sea, we came to a fork in the path which neither of us had anticipated. One arrow pointed to the beach at *La*

Fontelina and, about fifty yards in the opposite direction, with the rocks sloping toward the sea and some fishing nets left to dry on the ruins of an ancient Roman wall, another arrow marked the way to the beach known as *da Luigi*.

Dante studied the intersection as he would a compelling challenge that might present hidden obstacles.

"Which way?" he asked, at last.

"*La Fontelina*," I said. "I like the way it faces those enormous rocks. What are they called?"

"The *Faraglioni*."

So we ventured north, seduced by the colossal rocks, the iridescent sea, the splendour of a cloudless sky, the umbrella pines, the crickets.

On the last turn of our descent, where the path abruptly ended and gave way to the rocks that sloped down to the sea, we came upon a young woman lying on her back, asleep on a blue towel that protected her from the rock. It was not so much the beauty of her features that had drawn my eyes, but the complete abandon of her body against the craggy profile of rock. She resembled a nymph seduced by the embrace of the sun.

Dante had seen her, too, and he raised his eyebrows at me with an appraising look. We had both come to a stop, as if stunned, here, on this hot rock before this creature who boasted the firm voluptuous body of a woman in her twenties.

Other beachgoers walked back and forth on the path, but Dante and I remained rooted to the spot, staring at the thick cascade of dark hair with gingery steaks, the long eyelashes, the elegant nose, the prominent cheekbones, the sensuous contour of her mouth – the upper lip fuller than the other.

"Christ! If that isn't a gorgeous female," Dante whispered, so as not to disturb her.

"And brainy," I added in the same tone, catching a glimpse of Moravia's *La Bella Vita* propped against her satchel on the rock.

Unaccustomed to the voyeuristic pleasure of spying on a sleeping nymph, we remained unable to go forward or draw back.

Until Dante said, "You know, Trev. A sleeping woman is like a trout. She scares easily."

"So?"

"So I propose that we wake her up without startling her."

"We?" I said, and added, "No sharing. She's either yours or mine."

"Well, in that case, if you're so magnanimous –"

"Like hell," I cut him off. "Chance, I think will determine this."

"Chance? What the hell do you mean?"

"Let's break the pattern. Change our technique. I'm sick of our rules. I'd like the rest of my life to be determined by the toss of a coin."

Dante scowled. It was clear he saw me in the role of a loser who refused to admit defeat. But to his credit, he pulled out his silver dollar (the lucky one he always carried from childhood).

"We'll flip, shall we?" he asked.

"Heads," I said.

Descending a short distance from the young woman, Dante tossed the coin high in the air and stretched out his hand in an elaborate effort to catch it as it came down. But the coin eluded his grasp, flipped and flopped on the stone, then slid into a crevice between the rocks.

"Shit!" This from both of us as we dropped to our knees and stared at the glint of metal in the unreachable darkness.

"Shall I poke it loose?" Dante asked.

"With what?" I said.

"A stick, a twig, anything. I see something over there."

It was a straw someone had discarded. Dante grabbed it and carefully inserted it into the narrow opening. Prodded, the coin made a scratchy sound against the rock, scrambled upwards for a split second, and disappeared into the crack.

"Now what?" Dante said.

"I don't think it matters," I told him.

"Of course it matters. That was my lucky coin."

"Look. You'll see what I mean."

No surprise, was it? While the two Casanovas scrounged for a solution, the nymph had disappeared.

THIRTY-TWO

July 8, 2004

I stopped at Dante's flat on my way back home from a gallery in response to an urgent message he had left on my mobile. I found him throwing a pair of jeans, T-shirts, sweaters, socks and underwear into an old suitcase. His Nikon D80, batteries, and the pad where he jotted down ideas for the "iconic shot" had been packed into the duffel bag he carried with him.

"What the hell are you doing?" I asked.

"We're off to Naples."

"Naples, Italy?"

"Yeah," he said. "From there, we're taking the ferry to the island of Capri. You've heard about it, haven't you? Near the coast of Sorrento?"

"I know where Capri is. But what are we doing there? Turning into a pair of gigolos?"

"That's hypothetical. What's certain is our assignment with the *Corriere della Sera* which I got thanks to my good friend Franco Nicolini."

"Do I know him?"

"No. But you know *me*. So you're coming along. We are shooting the *Mare Moda* in Capri."

"The what?"

"Fashion of the sea. Gorgeous females wearing tiny bikinis."

"He closed the drawers and started to lock his suitcase. "Come on," he said. "Don't be difficult. Go home and pack. We're leaving in a few hours."

I had an urge to laugh, to ignore him, to taunt him about the assignment. When did Dante ever rope me into his life except to show off his genius?

"I'm impressed by the royal *we*," I said. "But what, exactly, will I be doing except following you around like a poodle?"

"Damn!" he yelled. "So bloody ungrateful. God save me from idiots posing as arrogant art dealers."

But, despite the row, he secured my passage to Naples, my hovercraft ride to Capri and my stay (all expenses paid) at the prestigious *Quisisana* Hotel.

* * *

"There," Dante said, as we admired the panoramic view from the gardens of Augustus. "What do you think of the contrast?"

"Magnificent," I said, taking in the vegetation that surrounded us high above the cliffs of the Marina Piccola.

That same day, I suggested to Dante that I roam around the island while he shot the collections, knowing that he'd be absorbed. But even such arduous discipline stopped at sunset when Dante joined me, either alone or with an assistant, on the terrace of the hotel for a *Bellini* (the delicious drink made of peach juice and champagne).

So it was not until the last day of the shoot, when the models were packing up to return to Milan, that the two of us were enjoying breakfast while arguing about the epic journey of Pope John Paul II.

"He's building up a legend for himself," I said. "Which is what Popes do."

"Nonsense," Dante argued. "He's genuinely concerned about all the misery in the world."

"As a moral arbiter, what else can he do? Unlike most of us who don't give a fig about the poor in Darfur."

"Never mind, Trev. Let's assume the Papacy is a job very few people are worthy of."

This brought the discussion to an abrupt end. I had a few hours to kill before meeting Dante for a farewell party in Naples that evening. After a leisurely lunch and a bottle of local wine, I made a visit to Tiberius Palace, where the shrill crowing of an invisible rooster disturbed the silence of the ruins.

When evening fell, I was quite ready to meet Dante at the Neapolitan night spot, *Tentazione*, a converted warehouse on Via Camerelle, enticingly named to whet the appetite of its patrons.

"What's all that smoke?" I asked the taxi driver, as we approached via Camerelle from the port.

But the man wasn't listening to me. He had turned up the volume on his car radio and seemed alarmed by what he heard.

"*Fuoco*," he said at last, as he squeezed into a chaotic line of vehicles making a U turn away from our destination.

"Fire? Where?" I asked.

"*Discoteca*."

"Which one?"

"*Tentazione*."

"Please keep going. I need to get there."

"*Mi dispiace*," he said, stopping the car and signalling me to get out.

Which I did. Quickly. The way I had always

imagined desperate people moved. Not thinking. Barely breathing. Just running. Glancing at the red glow in the sky while making frantic calculations about how long it would take me to get there.

The police had cordoned off the entrance to Via Camerelle, but they were unable to control the panicked men and women running away from the fire. I backed away in fear as I watched a wall collapse and come tumbling down onto the pavement.

If Dante were inside, the heat would make it impossible to get anywhere near him. Chivalry was forgotten as the flames seized me in their spell. *Run*, I said to myself. *Get away while there's still time.*

Too late. As I was thinking this, the street was blocked by the enormous bulk of four fire engines, their twirling red lights still on. About a dozen firemen poured out, their hoses unfurled, and began fighting the wall of fire, sending sheets of water to douse it down.

And then, the sky above my head was no longer red but grey. And hot. Like warm fog. Still I remained motionless, distrustful of combustion. How fast did it burn? For how long? Could the flames flare up again?

I realized I was talking to myself, asking questions and providing answers in a desperate effort to remain calm. Clouds of smoke rose before me, but the fire had been put out. The firemen were carrying out their equipment, getting ready to leave.

When I next moved, I heard the sound of my own footsteps going forward into the lounge, crunching the splintered glass scattered over the floor.

I yelled, "Dante!" and thought I heard a muffled cry from somewhere near a stairwell.

The air was thick with smoke, making it difficult to breathe. I was beginning to choke when I glimpsed an ice bucket wedged against the bar wall, a wet napkin dripping from it. I plucked it, held it against my face, and kept walking among pieces of burnt linoleum, broken bottles and chunks of masonry.

And that's when I saw him. Slumped on the ground with his back against the wall, his legs folded at a crooked angle and lying in a puddle of black water.

I rushed to him, knelt by his side and stared at his red arms, plucked hairless, and his teeth, chattering as if he were freezing cold.

"You hurt?" I asked.

He groaned, "Yeah," and pointed at his arms

and chest, then closed his eyes and said nothing more, as if the whole thing was too complicated to explain.

Though he was covered in soot, I could see that the skin on his arms looked ugly and raw. And the front of his shirt seemed stuck to his chest.

"Dante," I said. "We have to get out of here."

"Yeah."

"Can you put your arm around my shoulder?"

He tried. He flung his arm around me, but it dribbled down and he sank back onto the floor.

"Try again," I said.

He did. He reached out for my shoulder as I pulled him up and held him against me. He felt as if loaded with stones. But this time we kept our balance and hobbled across the room toward the exit.

"Hey, over here!" I screamed, spotting two paramedics rushing away with an empty stretcher.

Astonishingly they heard me, stopped, turned around and came back.

"*Adesso! Subito!*" they yelled, lifting Dante away from my shoulder and strapping him onto the stretcher.

"May I go with him?" I asked one of the paramedics.

"*Mi dispiace,*" he said, shaking his head.

"Where are you taking him?"

"*Ospedale*."

"Which one?"

"*Santa Maria di Napoli*."

I stooped to get close to Dante's ear. "Listen," I said. "I'll go back to the hotel, get your stuff, and meet you at the hospital."

I stopped watching them drive away in an ambulance when I heard the warehouse rumbling crazily behind me. *Time to get out*, I groaned, a hoarse whisper that scratched my gullet as if swallowing sandpaper, and then at last a portion of the ceiling began to cave in and an Englishman shouted, "Look out!"

His fear kindled my own. I overcame the terrible fatigue which had descended over me and told myself I had to run.

I leaped ahead, wiping away the ashes and dust that were blinding me, and kept running, struggling with my own exhaustion, a paralysing weakness that threatened to choke my breath and turn my legs into a heap of rags.

On the port, the wind had dropped, leaving behind a strong acrid smell.

"Is the *aliscafo* crossing over to Capri?" I asked.

"*Sempre*," the sailor answered with a sympathetic look at my dismal appearance, and added in heavily accented English, "Always. God willing. Neptune willing. We cross."

At that moment the plaintive whine of a foghorn hastened the late arrivals into the hover-craft.

As we moved away from the pier, I had a sudden sense of relief. The boat would cross over to Capri. Dante's burnt skin would heal. And, before rushing back to Naples, I would have a triple martini on the terrace of my hotel.

Epilogue

EPILOGUE

June 21, 2005

"There is a story – of dubious authenticity – that fishermen in the island of Procida like to tell about a mermaid who was so in love with a sailor that she capsized his vessel and dragged him down to the bottom of the sea, so that she alone could claim him and no other mermaid –"

The ringing of the bell at the gate startled Piero Giordano, who sat in a warm corner of the kitchen, absentmindedly sipping his morning coffee and listening to his favourite radio programme, *Tales of the Sea*, without paying attention to the words.

When the bell rang again, he rose anxiously and headed for the gate. Could it be news from London? A message from Detective McAndrews? But his sister, Flaminia, had already crossed over from her own room at the back of the house and was opening the gate.

The silence that greeted the visitor was vast. Strange. Broken by the joyous cry, "*Madonna*!"

He moved, quick as a lizard, almost stumbling over the step that led to the main room, his legs shaking, his arms stretched out to embrace Antonia, who appeared to his old eyes like a smudge of shadow against the sunlight.

"Hello, Father."

He meant to say, "*Ciao, bambina,*" but the words were stuck in his gullet, tight as the reef knot he fastened on his ropes.

By the time there were no more tears to shed, Flaminia had gone into the kitchen to get a breakfast tray for Antonia, and Piero's relief had shifted to curiosity.

"Where have you been for one whole week?" he asked.

"In London, hiding in a houseboat," Antonia said.

"A houseboat!"

"One of many along the Thames. I was lucky it was empty. And lucky I had my wallet and passport, or I wouldn't be here."

"Hiding from whom?"

"Trevor. I was afraid he would kill me. He was very, very angry."

"Couldn't you call the police?"

"There was no phone in the houseboat. I was too afraid to go out."

If anything was remarkable at all, it was not the chaos in Piero's mind, but the sense of calm, the certainty that Antonia, however shaken and bruised, had survived.

"The police said you were lost in –" he started.

"I wasn't *lost*," she said. "Trevor left me there to drown. And I almost did. The current dragged me a short way toward the canal, but I was able to cling to the root of a tree and pull myself out."

"Why were you in the water?"

"I was trying to rescue my dog. But I lost him. I don't know what happened to him."

Giving her a patient smile, Piero attempted to sort out the loose ends in his mind.

"Are you saying that Trevor was there the whole time?" he asked.

"Yes," Antonia said.

"Why didn't he help you?"

"It's a long story, Father. I'll tell you some day. And perhaps –"

At that moment Flaminia came back with a tray of steaming *caffè latte*, hot bread and homemade apricot jam.

"Eat," she said. "You must be hungry."

Antonia began to devour the food, shovelling chunks of bread and jam into her mouth.

"Don't eat so fast," Piero said. "You haven't escaped an angry husband to choke on a piece of bread."

Halfway through her breakfast, Antonia looked up and asked, "Have the police caught Trevor?"

"Not yet. I spoke to Detective McAndrews yesterday. He thinks Trevor may try to get away."

"Where would he go?"

"As far as he can get, I suppose."

"What about Danilo?"

"He's out of jail."

"Jail?"

"They suspected *him*. Not Trevor. But he's out now. Looking for you in London. I will call him and let him know you're here."

Antonia smiled. When she did, the heaviness in Piero's heart began to lift.

"I waited for you in London as long as I could," he explained. "But Detective McAndrews encouraged me to go. He said I'd better off waiting at home."

"He was wrong," Flaminia said. "Your father carried his anguish wherever he went. Couldn't eat. Couldn't sleep. All he did was read the newspapers –"

"And pray," Piero interrupted her. "I prayed so much, Antonia. I prayed in church, in the fields, in front of the shrine that holds your mother's photograph. I prayed that God would keep you safe."

"Thank you, Father."

"I told everyone who was willing to listen that I believe in miracles. And here you are, Antonia. You're my miracle."

Tears were again running down his face. Antonia put down her tray, went over to him and hugged him.

"No need for tears," she said. "I'm ready to celebrate. Guess what I'd like for lunch."

"What?"

"Aunt Flaminia's *vermicelli* with sautéed clams."

"And a bottle of *Brunello di Montalcino*," Piero said.

"And *torta* Caprese," Aunt Flaminia concluded, as she rose and headed for the kitchen.

* * *

And so, Antonia's homecoming was indeed joyful and exuberant and worthy of the long road she had travelled to get there.

Of Trevor himself, it was only known that there was a search warrant for his arrest, on charges of attempted murder. An Englishman fitting his description had been seen walking barefoot through the wet sand of a beach in Wellington, New Zealand. When a beachcomber approached him for a light, he had collected his sandals and his towel, and disappeared.

A few matrons in the market square of Anacapri raised disapproving eyebrows when Danilo arrived at the Giordano household. What was he doing there? Was Antonia two-timing her husband before the very eyes of the village?

As for Cappuccino, his fate remained undetermined. Inspector Fielding assumed that he had drowned. But Sergeant Dale, who believed that a hopeful outlook was his duty, was convinced the dog had paddled to safety and found himself another home.